BATMAN & ROBIN™

NOVELIZATION BY
MICHAEL JAN FRIEDMAN

BASED ON THE SCREENPLAY BY
AKIVA GOLDSMAN

WARNER BROS. PRESENTS

A JOEL SCHUMACHER FILM ARNOLD SCHWARZENEGGER GEORGE CLOONEY CHRIS O'DONNELL UMA THURMAN ALICIA SILVERSTONE "BATMAN & ROBIN" MICHAEL GOUGH PAT HINGLE ELLE MACPHERSON

MUSIC BY ELLIOT GOLDENTHAL EXECUTIVE PRODUCERS BENJAMIN MELNIKER and MICHAEL E. USLAN BASED UPON BATMAN CHARACTERS CREATED BY BOB KANE FOR DC COMICS SCREENPLAY BY AKIVA GOLDSMAN PRODUCED BY PETER MACGREGOR-SCOTT

DIRECTED BY JOEL SCHUMACHER

WWW.BATMAN-ROBIN.COM

WARNER BROS.
A TIME WARNER ENTERTAINMENT COMPANY
©1997 Warner Bros. All Rights Reserved.

WARNER BOOKS

A *Warner* Book

First published in Great Britain in 1997 by
Warner Books

Batman created by Bob Kane

Cover design by Don Puckey

A CIP catalogue record for this book
is available from the British Library.

ISBN 0 7515 2001 2

Printed and bound in Great Britain by
Clays Ltd, St Ives plc

Warner Books
A Division of
Little, Brown and Company (UK)
Brettenham House
Lancaster Place
London WC2E 7EN

ACKNOWLEDGMENTS

Comic books have always been a big part of my life. Anyone with whom I grew up will tell you that. I was the kid with the prodigious stacks of funny books in my room, so big and so many I had little room for anything else.

That's why it was such a kick to write about two of comics' best-known icons, Batman and Robin. Besides, when it comes to depth of character and dramatic potential, it doesn't get any better than these two.

For the opportunity to swing through the canyons of Gotham, and for a helping hand along the way, I owe a debt of gratitude to Betsy Mitchell and Wayne Chang at Warner Aspect, and to Charles Kochman and his associates at DC Comics. Without these people this book would not and could not have happened.

I'd also like to express my appreciation to Scott Peterson, Darren Vincenzo, and Jordan B. Gorfinkel, who toil on DC's Batman publications, for their support and unerring insights; and to Bat-guru Dennis O'Neil, for his visionary role in redefining the Dark Knight over the years.

Kudos to Akiva Goldsman for his witty and fast-paced script, which I trust will be a witty and fast-paced film. Lastly, I thank you, the reader—without whose enthusiasm the Bat would long ago have ceased to prowl.

PROLOGUE

A storm was coming.

Eight-year-old Bruce Wayne could feel it in the biting coldness of the air as he and his parents emerged from the movie theater. He could feel it in the way the hair prickled on the back of his neck.

And in case he still harbored some doubt, it was there in the pinkish-gray cast of the sky and the way the wind swirled in front of the theater, driving orphaned newspaper pages and brightly colored candy-bar wrappers in the ghostly blue light of the streetlamps.

The boy felt himself shiver and pulled up the collar of his coat. He wasn't the only one doing that, either. Everyone coming out of the theater was bundling up. Even the pigeons seemed agitated, eager to get to whatever shelter they could find.

A storm was coming, and everything in the world seemed to know it.

"Did you like the movie?" his mother asked.

Bruce turned to her, forgetting the chill for a moment as he basked in the glow of her smile. In the gray of her eyes. His mother was beautiful. He was proud of her for that.

"Yes," he said. "I liked it a *lot*."

Bruce felt a hand on his shoulder, strong but gentle—his father's hand. The boy smiled at the sense of assurance it gave him. With a hand like that on his shoulder, he could do anything. Take any risk, no matter how great.

"Of course he liked it," Bruce's father observed. "How could a youngster his age *not* have liked it?" He winked at the boy above his dark moustache. "What could be more thrilling than the snap of a cape and the flash of a blade and wide-eyed terror on the face of some villain?"

Bruce nodded, warming to the subject. "Uh-huh. And the way he marked him with a *Z*. That was cool, too." He would never forget that lightning slash of Zorro's sword point—or the sense that the bad guys had been shamed for what they'd done.

"Of course," Bruce's father added, "it wasn't just his flashing blade that carried the day." He tapped his temple with his forefinger. "It was what Zorro had up here." He pointed to his chest, beneath his woolen coat. "And in here. That's what made him a hero."

"Such wisdom," his wife gibed good-naturedly.

Bruce's father grunted. "I married *you*, my dear. If that's not a sign of wisdom, I'd like to know what *is*."

"Flatterer," his mother chuckled.

"Just calling them the way I see them."

Bruce liked it when his parents talked that way in front of him. It made him feel grown up. He wanted to say something clever, too, but he couldn't think of anything.

Suddenly, he felt a drop on his face. It was colder than it should've been, colder than rain had a right to be. *Sleet*, he thought.

"Great," said his father, wincing as he came to the same conclusion. "Who expected this so early in the year? And leave it to me to park so far from the theater."

"It's all right," said Bruce's mother, though she frowned a little as she watched the sleet catch the light from the streetlamps. "Honestly, Thomas. A little weather never hurt anyone."

They walked down the block, away from the theater and the emerging crowd, past a dirty stone building with wrought-iron bars over its first-floor windows. Looking up, Bruce saw a stone figure with the face and wings of an eagle sticking out from a third-floor cornice.

The figure seemed to leer at him, to grin like the Devil as the sleet grew heavier. Looking away, he let his parents bustle him along the sidewalk.

The boy had no idea how to get back to their car. He didn't know the city because he very seldom got a chance to visit it. Mostly, he played on the sprawling grounds of his family's estate.

That's what had made this trip to a downtown theater so special. That and the fact that his dad had come along.

After all, Thomas Wayne was the best surgeon in town. He took on only the toughest cases, the kind no one else would touch. But his responsibility to his patients didn't end in the operating room.

He had to make sure someone was around if they needed help afterward—if there was an emergency. And there weren't many other doctors skilled enough to cover for him.

Bruce and his parents reached the corner, turned, and went up the avenue. They saw dark, sky-spanning bridges and mighty office spires, the tops of which were swallowed by the storm.

Then they turned again. They passed a tall, gray church, a tiny food store with a Spanish sign, and a freight entrance to a dress factory and hurried on, the wind stinging Bruce's cheeks.

Past more buildings. More shops, some of them shuttered. At some point, the boy realized he and his parents were the only people he could see in any direction.

But it was okay, he told himself. As long as he had his

parents on either side of him, he had nothing to worry about. It was an adventure, that's all. An adventure he could tell the kids about in school the next day.

At one point, Bruce thought he heard the scrape of footsteps on the sidewalk behind them. But when he glanced over his shoulder, he didn't see anything. He chalked it up to his imagination.

By the time they reached the next corner, it was really coming down—a hissing, whispering barrage that slid past his collar and sent ice water down his neck. His parents tugged him along, no doubt as blinded as the boy was by the sheeting deluge and just as eager to get out of it.

They rushed down the avenue and then up another street. And then stopped. Bruce's father looked around, his breath making a vapor trail.

"Where's the car?" he asked.

The boy looked around, too, as if he could shed some light on the problem. But of course, he couldn't.

His mother shook her head. "I don't know. But if we don't find it soon, Bruce is going to catch a cold."

"Nonsense, Martha," said his father. "You don't catch a cold from the weather." But the lines in his face showed that he was concerned. "Not to worry," he said in a softer voice, hugging the boy to him with one arm and his wife with the other. "It must be on the next street."

But halfway up the next street, Bruce's father began muttering under his breath. "It's not here either. It's got to be the next one."

"Thomas . . ." said his mother.

Then his father pointed. Following the gesture, Bruce saw the alley mouth that opened across the street from them. It was shadowy, full of garbage cans and windswept debris.

"I remember now," said his father. "There was an alley right nearby. The car is just on the other side."

"Are you sure?" asked the boy's mother.

His father nodded, his hair and moustache crusted with sleet. "I'm sure. Come on."

He led them across the street and into the alley. The place was dark and foreboding and full of puddles, but Bruce could see a streetlight at the other end. With his mother on one side of him and his father on the other, he put his head down and made his way against the wind.

It's okay, the boy assured himself. *It's almost over. We'll be home before we know it and there'll be a fire in the—*

Suddenly, he heard a voice ring out. As it echoed in the narrow confines of the alley, Bruce turned and saw a man standing behind them. A man in a cap and a leather jacket. He had something in his hand.

"What?" asked the boy's father. Apparently, he hadn't heard what the man said either.

The man came closer. And Bruce realized what he'd seen in the man's hand. It was a gun.

Bruce felt a terrible *chill*—an arctic cold that seemed to reach into his bowels and freeze them solid. His heart beat heavily in his chest, a trapped animal desperately trying to get out.

"What do you want?" Thomas Wayne demanded.

There was a moment of silence. The boy listened closely, expecting the man to answer. But the man didn't open his mouth.

Instead, a flare of blue-white fire came out of his gun— and there was a crack. Like the sound of Zorro's whip, but louder. As loud as thunder splitting the heavens.

Bruce's father grunted. As if mired in slow motion, the boy looked at him—saw his father double over in pain. Then he fell to the ground, still clutching at himself.

No, thought Bruce, his mind refusing to accept the evidence of his eyes. *No. Not my* father . . .

Then there was another peal of thunder. And as he watched, horrified, his mother went spinning away from him, the string of pearls around her neck breaking free and scattering over the pavement.

Mother? he screamed inwardly. And then, even more frantically, more disbelievingly, he screamed it aloud.

"Mother?"

But she couldn't answer. Martha Wayne just lay there, her blood pooling on the darkly glistening ground around her, her arm stretched toward the equally motionless body of her husband.

Bruce's hands climbed to his mouth, became fists as the man with the gun reached inside his father's coat and took something off his mother's wrist. The boy yelled something at him, he didn't know what, caught in a tide of horror and anger and despair.

Then the gunman was gone. Bruce approached his parents' bodies, touched them—felt the absence of life and hope and sank down between them on the hard, wet ground.

In the distance, he heard footsteps. Clear and sharp, but retreating. Fading into nothingness. Then, after a time, there was another sound—the strident skirl of a siren, growing louder and louder, until it filled the whole world with its complaint.

He looked up at the whirling lights of a police car. Saw the policemen get out, guns drawn. Heard one of them call for an ambulance.

But it was too late. Bruce knew that.

It was cold, he thought. It was so *cold*. And now he was all alone in the storm.

Alfred stood by one of the immensely tall windows in the living room of Wayne Manor. He watched a forlorn flock of geese navigate an iron gray sky. Like so much of

Nature, the geese were retreating before the inevitable onset of winter.

A tiny figure was standing in the snow-dusted field outside the mansion, looking up at the geese as Alfred was. But despite the chill, he wasn't retreating. Not from winter or anything else.

"Mr. Pennyworth?"

The butler turned and regarded the stout, balding gentleman sitting in the master's easy chair. Or at least, what *had* been the master's easy chair until a couple of miserable weeks ago. The man's cup sat on a coaster, which in turn sat on an eighteenth-century end table.

"More tea, sir?" Alfred asked.

"No," said the stout man. "Thank you. But you see what I'm saying, don't you? About the danger?"

"To Master Bruce," the butler replied.

"Precisely," said the stout man. "As you're aware, Mr. Pennyworth, I've treated a great many victims of severe psychological trauma. And in every case, the reaction to that trauma has been rather obvious.

"Sometimes, it takes the form of aggression—a desire to strike back at one's fate, if you will, often wildly and indiscriminately. In other instances, we see a withdrawal from life, a shoring up of the mind's defenses that in the extreme approaches catatonia. Or, as an alternative, the patient sinks into a deep morass of despair, afraid to ever again invest his love and trust in another human being."

"And yet?" Alfred responded. For an "and yet" seemed rather implicit in the psychiatrist's tone.

"And yet," the stout man went on, "none of these behaviors is observable in Master Bruce. To all outward appearances, he is a normal boy. Or at least, as normal as he was before the . . . er, incident." He blushed.

It was an awkward moment to be sure. After all, Alfred had been affected by the *incident* as well. True, he had served as the Waynes' butler only for a brief period of time, and had never expected to remain here for long. But by the time of their deaths, he had grown exceedingly fond of his employers, and he gathered that was evident in his behavior.

"Yes," Alfred said, doing his best to affect the psychiatrist's clinical tone. "The incident. Please continue."

The stout man folded his hands across his ample belly. "As I understand it, the boy has always been something of a loner. No steady playmates, no other child to whom he's been particularly close."

"True," the butler confirmed. "However, that was hardly anyone's choice. The vast majority of Master Bruce's schoolmates live on the other side of town, and it simply was not practical for him to engage in regular visits."

The psychiatrist smiled sympathetically. "I didn't mean to imply otherwise, Mr. Pennyworth. I'm only pointing out that the boy wasn't particularly gregarious to begin with, so one wouldn't look for him to be gregarious now." He paused. "As I say, normal. At least, on the outside."

"But not on the inside?" Alfred sighed.

The stout man's expression waxed more serious. "No. And therein lies his peril. You see, young Bruce may seem quite the stalwart, but there's still a child beneath that veneer of calm acceptance. A child who's experienced a greater trauma than you or I can ever comprehend."

Alfred glanced at the strangely resolute figure in the wintry field. The geese were gone now, but the boy was still staring at something.

"Don't be fooled, Mr. Pennyworth. The day will come when that veneer crumbles, and the boy reacts to the memory of his ordeal. Such matters may be postponed, but not indefinitely. And the longer this one is delayed, the greater the damage will be to his psyche."

Alfred nodded, his eyes still on the figure. "I see."

"Which makes it all the more important to encourage

young Bruce to come to grips with his fate. To open himself up to it and embrace it sooner rather than later, no matter how painful it may be for him."

The butler nodded again. "This, then, will be the course of your treatment? To bring his feelings about his parents' murder out into the open?"

"Yes. Otherwise, he may simply explode one day. And he may not be the only one hurt in that explosion."

Alfred swallowed at the prospect. "You've spoken of this with Master Bruce's uncle Philip?"

"I have," the stout man confirmed. "He says he values your opinion more than his own. You've lived with the boy day in and day out, he tells me, and he has not."

The butler considered his young charge. He knew the stout man was right. There was a great deal of pain contained in that tiny vessel. Somehow, it had to be let out.

"Tell me," he said. "What is your prognosis?"

The psychiatrist paused. "Even in the simplest cases, it's difficult to say. We're not talking about a broken leg or a torn muscle here. We're talking about a wound to the soul."

"Still," Alfred pressed, "how do you think this will all come out? Off the record, if you prefer."

Another pause. "I am not terribly optimistic," the stout man admitted. "But I assure you, I will do my best."

The butler frowned. It didn't seem he had much choice in the matter. Before his death, Thomas Wayne had spoken highly of the stout man. If Master Bruce was going to receive treatment, it might as well come from someone his father had known and respected.

"Very well," Alfred said at last. "Please let me know when you would like to see Master Bruce. I will make certain he is present."

"Excellent," the psychiatrist remarked. With a bit of an effort, he got to his feet. "Just one more thing, Mr. Pennyworth."

Alfred looked at him. "Yes?"

"Forgive me, but Mr. Wayne once described your employment here as temporary. He mentioned that your first love is the theater—and that you hope to return to it one day."

"It had occurred to me," Alfred conceded.

The stout man's brow furrowed. "Normally, it would be none of my business—but I ask out of concern for young Bruce. He's already lost the two most important people in the world to him. I don't know how close you and he have become, but right now you're the only real constant in his life."

"And if I have any intentions of leaving, it would be a good idea to speak of them now," Alfred said, picking up on the thought. "So I can be eased out of the boy's life."

The psychiatrist eyed him. "That's the gist of it, yes."

The butler glanced again at the boy. He was still standing there in the field, his eyes fixed on only-God-knew-what, the weight of the world on his narrow little shoulders.

"No," said Alfred. "It may once have been true that I considered myself a transient in this house. But it is true no longer. I intend to remain here for the duration."

However long that may be, he added inwardly, matching his resolve to that of the lonely child outside.

A teenage Bruce Wayne stood in the shadows of a gnarled and ancient oak, out of sight of the full moon, and surveyed the athletic field that sprawled before him in the frosty blue light.

The university's academic buildings loomed behind it like dark, hoary gods brooding over an ancient battleground. But it was only a battleground in the most figurative sense, in the sense of clashing athletes. From a literal perspective, it was just a meadow with an oval track in the center of it.

The track was deserted this night except for a solitary figure in a navy blue sweat suit, loping easily over the clay red composite surface. Large but agile-looking, just shy of his twenty-fourth birthday, he kept up a ground-eating pace without much effort—stride after stride, minute after minute, lap after lap.

And he wasn't even pushing himself. He was just warming up.

A casual observer might not have known that. But Bruce knew it. He knew all the man's best footrace times by heart. Of course, running wasn't the man's only forte. He was also a world-class competitor in the javelin toss, the hurdles, the pole vault, and several other events.

That was what it took to become the premier decathlete on the planet. One had to be among the elite in a great many areas of endeavor.

Bruce knew a lot more about the man in the sweat suit. How he had been born in a small, picturesque town in Europe, which accounted for his slight accent. How his mother had been an Olympic-caliber speed skater and his father a prominent biologist. How they had moved to the United States shortly after their son turned two. And a good deal more, some of which the man himself might even have forgotten.

But none of it was particularly important right now. Only the ease with which the man flowed around the oval—only the speed he mustered without breaking a sweat. Bruce watched, eager to learn. Eager to add the man's posture and rhythms and expertise to his collection.

That was the way he had come to think of himself—as a collector, as someone who took a little from here and a little from there, acquiring and assembling and stockpiling. He'd been at it since he was fourteen. And though he was nearly twenty now, his collection was still woefully incomplete.

He was like a squirrel, he thought, hoarding nuts for a long, cold winter. But the squirrel in his analogy had an advantage—it knew what to expect. It knew what it would need to survive.

Bruce didn't. So he collected everything he thought he *might* need, no matter how offbeat or esoteric.

He learned martial arts—and patience—from a wizened old man in Korea. Street smarts from the legendary manhunter Ducard in France. Fencing in the Soviet Union and auto racing in the streets of Rome.

He became fluent in several different languages and obtained a working knowledge of several more. He studied chemistry and biology, criminology and computer design with a dozen teachers in a dozen different places.

All in the hope that when the time came, he'd be ready. He'd be equipped for the kind of mission no one had undertaken in the history of humankind.

After a while, the man on the track slowed down. To a jog. To a walk. Then he crossed the short-cropped field described by the track and approached a narrow runway made of the same composite material.

There was an elongated sandpit at the end of the runway. Someone had raked it recently, taking out the footprints that had dug into it and bulldozed the sand around. But it wouldn't stay that way for long, Bruce mused.

As he looked on, the man in the sweat suit took up a position at the head of the runway. He drew a deep breath, then let it out. It turned ghostly in the cold, bracing air.

The man rocked once and then deliberately, purposefully, began to run the length of the runway. Before long, he was sprinting, going full tilt. When he neared the end of the runway, the man leaped and launched himself high into the air.

For a moment or two, he seemed to be riding an imaginary bicycle, his arms and legs pumping furiously. Then he thrust his feet out ahead of him and came to a sliding stop in the sandpit.

The man made a face, obviously less than satisfied. Picking himself up, he left the sandpit and retraced his steps to try it again.

That's when Bruce decided to show himself. Leaving the obscuring shadow of the oak, he jogged out onto the track. The man turned but didn't pay him much attention. It was a university track, after all. Students ran it all the time, even at this late hour.

Bruce contained himself, just as the man had but even more so, keeping his pace to little more than a jog. All the while, however, he remained intent on the man in the sweat suit as he completed jump after jump.

After what seemed like enough time, Bruce slowed down and walked over to the runway. The man was staring at it, rubbing a muscle between his shoulder blades. He still seemed dissatisfied.

Bruce checked out the footprints in the sandpit. He looked up and smiled appreciatively.

"Not bad," he said. "Not bad at all."

The man turned to him. He had prominent cheekbones and a sweep of long, brown hair that fell almost to the bridge of his nose. And eyes like pale blue ice chips.

"Not good," the man replied, with just a hint of an accent. Then he amended his statement, perhaps fearing that it sounded immodest. "Not good *enough*, I mean. I can do better."

Bruce paced off the distance from the man's footprints to the beginning of the sandpit. "Wait a minute," he said. "This could be a world's—"

"A world's record," the man finished for him. "Yes. I know. But there are going to be a lot of records broken in the next year or so. A lot of good people coming up. I want to be ready for them."

Bruce pretended to stare at the man for a moment. "Hey, aren't you . . . that guy, that athlete . . . ?" He pretended to fumble for the name, though he knew it almost as well as his own.

"Victor Fries," said the man.

Bruce pointed to him. "Yeah . . . Victor Fries. You won the Olympics last year. I saw you on television."

"Not the whole Olympics." Fries chuckled good-naturedly. "As I recall, it was just the decathlon."

Bruce chuckled too. "Well, it's a pleasure to meet you." He offered his hand, and the other man took it.

"The pleasure is mine," said Fries, polite in an Old World kind of way. His grip was strong—just what Bruce would have expected from someone who could toss a hammer as far as Fries could.

Bruce considered the sandpit again. Those jumps Fries had made *were* pretty impressive. "So what's your secret?" he asked abruptly—in the manner of someone purely curious, with no agenda at all.

The question took the man by surprise. "Secret?"

"Yeah," said Bruce. "I figure anyone who can jump as far as you can has to have a secret. Some little . . . I don't know. Some kind of *edge*."

Fries shrugged. "I have an approach, I guess. Everyone does." He smiled. "But how do I know you're not a decathlete in the making, trying to take my title away?"

Bruce laughed. "Yeah, that's me. The world-class decath . . . decath . . . what'd you call it?"

"Decathlete," said the other man.

Bruce grunted. "Yeah. Decathlete."

Under the circumstances, Fries couldn't help but see how absurd the idea was. If he only knew, thought Bruce. If Fries had any inkling of how hard his young admirer had worked to make his body a perfect machine . . .

"Well," said Fries, "it's like this." He used his hand to indicate his imaginary progress along the runway. "You run, you jump, you keep your balance as you sail through the air. All very important. But to me, the key is the landing." He turned to Bruce. "In other words, whether or not you choose to make one."

Bruce narrowed his eyes. "What do you mean?"

The decathlete shrugged. "I know it's going to sound strange, but I don't land—not when it's a really good jump. I just *hang* there."

"But you land eventually," Bruce pointed out.

"Not really. I mean, sure, gravity brings me down after a while. But not as quickly as it has a right to." The man's ice-chip eyes glazed over—but only for a fraction of a second. "Then I realize the jump is over, and I'm back on the ground."

Part of Bruce, the part that had audited courses with the world's foremost physicists and mathematicians, wanted to insist it was all hogwash. Forward progress on a flat plane was a function of momentum, friction, and gravity. Nothing else.

But another part of him, the part that had studied psychology and belief systems and arcane philosophies, argued that the mind could do things the body on its own could not. And that part of him felt the trip to this place had been worthwhile.

"You just hang there," he said.

"That's it," Fries confirmed.

Bruce nodded. "I'll remember that."

And he would. He would file it away with all the other bits and pieces of wisdom he'd accumulated in his travels. And someday, he was sure, he would find a use for it.

Suddenly, he was aware of another presence in the vicinity of the track. He turned and saw a tall, slender, and decidedly female figure approaching from the direction of campus.

Even at a distance, Bruce could see how beautiful she was. How ethereal in the moonlight, even in simple jeans and a woolen sweater. She didn't say anything. She just smiled and beckoned.

But not to him. To Fries.

Beside Bruce, the decathlete smiled the smile of a man in love. "Got to go," he said.

"What about all those challengers?" asked Bruce. "The ones who are out to take your title?"

Fries clapped Bruce on the shoulder. "Everyone's got his priorities, my friend. The decathlon is important to me, make no mistake. But not half as important as *she* is."

And with that, the man jogged across the field to meet his girlfriend. With all he'd read about Fries, Bruce would have known if she was the decathlete's wife.

As they met, they embraced. Fries swung her off her feet. Bruce felt like an intruder. He wanted to look away, to do the polite thing, but he couldn't take his eyes off them. They were a beautiful couple.

He wanted to be part of something like that. Wanted it in the worst way. But the kind of plans he had made left no room for romance. No room for permanent attachments of any kind.

He would be alone. Always alone. It was the path he had chosen, and he would remain faithful to it.

Bruce waited until Fries and his girlfriend had receded into the distance and disappeared among the baroque silhouettes of the university buildings. Then he lined himself up at the start of the runway.

Taking a deep breath, he hunkered down and took off. Running as fast as he could, he accelerated all the way to the end of the composite strip. Then he launched himself into space and bicycled high out over the sandpit.

Just as he was about to come to earth, he commanded himself to wait. To hang there instead. To deny gravity its due, if only for the slightest fraction of a second longer.

What's more, it worked. When Bruce's feet came down in the sand, they were just a few inches shy of Fries's best effort. Bruce didn't smile, but he came close. A few more jumps and he might have set a record himself.

But no one could know that. His ambitions, his goals, were still a secret. He wanted them to stay that way.

Getting up out of the sand, he brushed himself off and returned to the oak. Then he picked up the backpack he had left behind it, slung it over his shoulder, and moved on.

After all, he'd heard about a contortionist in Kansas City. And one never knew when such a talent might come in handy.

CHAPTER
1

Bruce Wayne pondered the trap laid out so cleverly in front of him.

Lobster thermidor. Wild mushroom risotto. Julienne of gingered carrots and zucchini. All tastefully arranged on his plate. And beside it a perfectly chilled glass of Château Lafitte Rothschild '56.

He turned to Dick Grayson, his ward, who sat around the corner from him at the long, polished dining-room table. "Cunning," he said.

Dick considered his own dinner and nodded appreciatively. "Dastardly is more like it."

Bruce closed his eyes and sampled the aroma of the lobster thermidor. "We should be working on the new vehicles. Putting them through their paces."

His ward grunted. "We *should* be doing that."

"But instead," said Bruce, "we've been maneuvered into . . . *this*."

"Yeah," Dick agreed. "Sitting down at the dinner table and eating a meal fit for a king." He tilted his head to indicate the kitchen door. "Even as we speak, he's probably in there whipping up a dessert—something to *really* throw us off schedule."

"Is there no end to the man's cruelty?" Bruce asked.

"None," Dick replied with grim certainty. "None at all."

"We could try to escape," Bruce suggested.

"For all the good it'll do us." Dick's eyes narrowed. "I think he's really got us this time."

The billionaire sighed. "So we resign ourselves to our fates? We give up without a fight?"

"Seems like the only intelligent thing to do."

"Right you are." Bruce unfolded his napkin and placed it on his lap. "Let's dig in."

He was just picking up his knife and fork when he caught a glimpse of something through the window. Turning to it, he saw a beam of light stabbing at the lowermost layer of clouds.

Where the light made contact, there was a black shape. The shape of a bat, its wings outstretched as if in flight. Bruce knew it all too well.

And since he'd come to live with the billionaire, Dick knew it, too. He followed Bruce's gaze, saw what he was looking at, then took a last, lingering look at his dinner.

"We go?" he asked. It wasn't really a question.

"We go," Bruce said, confirming it anyway.

Together, they put their napkins on the table and traversed the ample interior of Wayne Manor. Circumnavigating the magnificent central stairway, they made their way to the study at the far end of the house.

Inside it, there was a grandfather clock, its face open and exposed. It said 6:51. But Bruce reset its hands to 10:47—a time that had great significance for him. After all, it was the hour and minute at which his parents had died.

The clock swung aside, revealing itself as a disguised door. Beyond, there was a dimly lit cascade of stone stairs that wound down into what seemed like the bowels of the earth. Bruce descended with Dick right behind him, the clock door closing automatically in their wake.

Their footfalls echoed as they followed the winding of the stair. Finally, it deposited them on the floor of a cavern—a place where the stalagmites had long since been cleared away, but sharp stalactites still hung overhead.

A cavern where a huge copper penny gleamed under the glare of suspended lights. Where a vast array of computer consoles sat beneath three large screens, monitoring all that went on in nearby Gotham City and its environs.

This was the Batcave, known to only a few people in the entire world. Home to a creature of the night most people still didn't believe in. But Bruce Wayne believed.

He had to. He was that creature.

Crossing the floor of the cave, Bruce headed for his costume vault. Removing his clothes in semidarkness, the billionaire reached for the nearest of the several uniforms hanging in front of him.

Though it looked like black rubber, it was actually a suit of lightweight, flexible armor, molded to the contours of his body. There was a bat emblazoned on his chest, just like the bat he'd seen against the clouds.

He pulled on his boots, snapped his gauntlets into place, and whipped his cape over his shoulders. Then he took his yellow-gold Utility Belt off a rack, encircled his waist with it, and locked the buckle in front of him.

But for the moment, he was still Bruce Wayne. Still a man, no more and no less, until he included the final detail.

Reaching for the cowl that was attached to the neckline of his suit, he pulled it forward over his face. Suddenly, he felt it. He was transformed. Bruce Wayne was gone—in his place, a denizen of the night.

Batman.

As he emerged from his vault, he saw Robin do the same. The boy was wearing a new costume he and Alfred had been working on. Instead of the red tunic he had worn as a member of the Flying Graysons, Robin sported a red-bird insignia that spread across his chest and ran down the outside of his arms.

Batman grunted as he approached his computer array. "Nice suit. And today you are . . . ?"

"Nightwing," said Robin, joining him at the central console. "Scourge of darkest evil."

Taking a seat, Batman tapped into the police band, wanting to know what had prompted Commissioner Gordon to unleash the Bat-Signal. But with a part of his mind, he continued their banter.

"This is all about fashion for you, isn't it?"

Standing by his side, Robin leaned over the console and chuckled. "It's the gear," he said, with just a hint of irony in his voice. "Chicks go wild over the gear."

"I'll keep that in mind," Batman responded.

As Alfred descended the stairs into the Batcave, a tray of lobster-salad sandwiches and tea in hand, he sighed.

He had gotten used to the sight of a masked avenger sitting before the mighty Cray computers, his eyes glinting in the glare of a trio of oversize monitors, his cape catching the light of a dozen smaller surveillance screens situated on the opposite wall.

That is, Alfred had become accustomed to *one* such figure. But now there were *two* of them, God help him.

Two young men in masks and dark, molded body armor, ready to risk life and limb for a common purpose. A common cause. Or a common insanity, depending on how one looked at it.

Batman and Robin. Sworn enemies of the Gotham criminal underworld, impelled by fate and circumstance to aid the innocent and protect those who could not protect themselves.

And their fearsome accoutrements? Their dire appearances?

They were essential to the task of fighting crime—or so his employer had explained to him time and again. Criminals were a superstitious and cowardly lot in Master Bruce's estimate. Hence, the more imposing one's appearance, the more effective a crime fighter one could be.

At least, that was the theory.

Of course, neither Master Bruce nor Master Dick was inclined to tend to the *laundering* of their accoutrements. Nor could they entrust them to the local dry cleaner. That part in the Great Undertaking fell to Alfred.

Not that he was complaining. He *never* complained about how they were taking care of their clothes. Only about how they were taking care of *themselves*—or failing to, as the case might be.

Still descending, Alfred cleared his throat. "Taking back the night again, are we?"

His voice echoed through the immensity of the cavern, eliciting a whisper of wings from the swarms of bats in the outlying caves. They had retreated to those recesses when Master Bruce claimed this space as his own, and retreated still farther when he enlarged it recently.

The crime fighters turned to him. Only Robin smiled in his mask, which covered less of his face than Master Bruce's cowl.

"Hey, Al," he said, gracing the butler with a little wave.

"Indeed," said Alfred. Master Dick was the only one on earth who could call him that with impunity. "If I may ask, what is so interesting that it caused you to abandon my lobster thermidor?"

"Ten police cruisers," Batman said without looking up. "Frozen solid on the Gotham Expressway."

His protégé peered at the central monitor, reading the information scrolling by in a corner of it. "A giant drilling truck burrowing under the city," he added.

Robin was making an effort to affect the Batman's clipped, efficient rhythms. He was still falling short.

"Mr. Freeze," Batman concluded.

Robin nodded. "The Batcomputer tracks him heading for the Gotham Museum. What's there?"

Batman thought for a moment, the muscles rippling in his jaw. "The new antiquities exhibit. Including the Second Sun of the Sudan, on loan from the British Museum in London."

Robin laughed triumphantly. "Of course. He's going to steal that giant white diamond."

Batman shook his head. "No, Robin," he said with absolute certainty. "He's going to jail."

Before the echoes of his promise had died away, there was a blast of steam on the other side of the cave, the by-product of a powerful hydraulic system. As Batman strode toward it, the steam cleared and revealed a sleek, redesigned Batmobile resting on a huge metal pedestal.

He touched a stud on his Utility Belt and the hatch opened to admit him. With characteristic grace and agility, Batman swung inside and drew his cape in after him.

Alfred called out from the bottom of the stairs. "Do call if you're going to be late, sir. You know how I worry."

It was a joke between them. But there was a note of seriousness in it as well, and both of them knew it.

The Batmobile's turbo-charged engines roared, sending out one resounding echo after another. A moment later, the vehicle shot away through the stalactite-ridden arches of the cavern's access tunnel.

No sooner had it departed than the surface of the pedestal split open like the petals of a flower—revealing a sleek, turbo-charged motorcycle. It was Robin's bike, the Redbird.

Alfred called out again. "Drive carefully, Master Dick."

Robin winked at him with calculated abandon as he straddled the powerful machine. "Don't wait up, Al."

Then the Redbird's engine exploded into life, and the bike shot out through the tunnel after the Batmobile. Alfred watched it go until it was lost to darkness and distance.

He hated the idea of what they would face out there. But at the same time, he understood the desperate need for someone to face it. And the desperate need within Master Bruce and Master Dick that made them want the responsibility.

Suddenly, he felt an excruciating pain in his side—an agony so overwhelming it forced him to drop his tray of sandwiches and drinks. The cups of tea shattered on the hard rock floor of the cave, sending liquid flying in every direction.

Alfred himself staggered forward, barely able to support himself, and grabbed the edge of the massive computer console. His suffering went on for what seemed like forever. And he remained there, gasping for air, teeth clenched against it, until the pain at last began to subside.

My God, he thought. *My God.*

Still, he was glad neither Master Bruce nor Master Dick had been present to see his discomfort. Gathering himself on trembling legs, he took out a handkerchief to remove the sweat that had accumulated on his brow.

My God, he thought again.

Then he recovered his tray, got down on one knee, and began to pick up the shards of glass. After all, the Batcave was part of Wayne Manor—part of the home with whose care he was charged. And he wouldn't allow a mess to remain there one second longer than it absolutely had to.

Clayton Krupzic had ice water in his veins.

At least, that's what he liked to tell people back in Waumagansett Falls. "Nothing scares me," he'd add, impressing the hell out of the old geezers who liked to gather at the filling station. "Nothing in heaven or hell or on God's green earth."

But it was a hard thing for a farm boy like Clayton to prove. After all, the scariest thing in Waumagansett Falls was *him*, and after that it was his twin sister Coleen.

It got to the point where he'd go to other towns and pick fights on Saturday nights. But he didn't find much of a challenge in those places either. No one big enough, no one mean enough.

So as soon as he finished the twelfth grade, Clayton hightailed it for the big city—despite the warnings of everyone in town—and applied for a job in law enforcement.

Why not? Gotham didn't require a cop to attend any kind of academy. If you'd finished high school, it was considered a bonus. In fact, it made you detective material.

Trouble was, the Gotham Police Force was in the middle of some down-and-dirty budget cuts when he arrived. Someone suggested he go into security work until the department started hiring again.

At first, Clayton was too proud for that. He hadn't come to Gotham to be a rent-a-cop. But his pride lasted only until his savings ran out, which wasn't long at all. Then he had to look for a job—or face the prospect of going back home and working at the filling station.

Eventually, he found gainful employment at the Gotham Museum, a sprawling stone-and-glass palace set on the edge of Gotham's Central Park. Unfortunately, the work was even more boring than he'd feared. Just a lot of strolling through big, empty corridors with nobody but the mummies for company.

Oh, he saw some of the other guards sometimes at the stairways, their flashlights probing the darkness just like his. But that wasn't more than a half dozen times a night.

If not for the periodic walkie-talkie buzz from the main station, Clayton would've gone stark, raving nuts.

So it took him by surprise one night when the building began to shiver, and the air was split with a high-pitched whine.

At first, he thought it was an earthquake causing the commotion—even though there was no record of any earthquakes in Gotham's history. Then he heard the frantic voice of Sanchez, the old guy down on the first floor.

"It's drillin' up through the floor!" he wailed. "Ya better getcher butts down here!"

Clayton didn't think twice. He came running, though he was farther away than any of the other guards. He didn't know what the blazes Sanchez was talking about, but if there was some kind of action in the museum, he was determined to be in on it.

How else was he going to prove what he'd been saying all his life—about that ice water in his veins?

Clayton went down the stairs two at a time, heading for the first floor. By the time he rounded the World of Lizards exhibit, the high-pitched whining had stopped. So had Sanchez's calls for help.

Pouring it on, Clayton sprinted through the Hall of Man and Wonders of the Weather. Up ahead and around the bend, in the vicinity of the central rotunda, there was something going on. He could hear sounds, though he couldn't identify any of them.

Then he turned the corner and he saw what was happening. And it took his breath away—just as if he'd been belly-whomped with a milk bucket.

Inside the rotunda, the nose of a giant drilling truck was protruding through the rubble of the shattered museum floor. And everything—the mighty brontosaurus that dominated the rotunda and a host of other exotic antiquities—*everything* was covered in a layer of thick, blue ice.

Out of the corner of his eye, Clayton saw movement and

whirled to face it, gun in hand. Across the way, a case with a gigantic gem in it was beginning to glow. First blue, then white. And in a matter of a few seconds, the case exploded into a thousand flying fragments.

Through the storm of ice and glass, Clayton heard a peal of laughter. He traced it to its source.

Across the frozen floor. Past snow-covered mock-ups of Aztec ruins. Up the stone steps of a pyramidal altar.

To a tall, broad, silver-suited figure, holding aloft what looked like a massive bazooka—no doubt the weapon that had shattered the display case—in savage but silent celebration of his triumph.

There were heavy metal boots on his feet, heavy metal gauntlets on his forearms, and a heavy metal shell protecting his upper body. His transparent helmet revealed a bizarre, bluish countenance rimed with frost.

As if he could feel Clayton's gaze on him, the figure turned to face him. Eyes like ice chips focused on him, made him feel like an insect. *Less* than an insect. And suddenly, Clayton knew who the intruder was, though until now he'd only heard about him.

It was the villain known as Mr. Freeze.

But Freeze didn't look like a man. Gazing down haughtily from on high, holding his fearsome weapon aloft, he looked like some wintry god of evil—some high-tech monster hungering for his soul. And as much as Clayton tried to tell himself that was impossible, that such things didn't exist, his trembling knees were far from convinced.

"The Iceman cometh," Freeze intoned, in a voice as cold and flat and lifeless as the arctic wastes.

Then, almost as an afterthought, he cracked a smile at his little joke. And turned in the direction of the Aztec ruins.

Following his stare, Clayton saw something he had missed the first time—something that had been added to the exhibit. Three dark-suited figures, frozen in various postures with guns in their hands.

Sanchez and the others. Iced solid before they could interfere with Freeze's plans. Clayton grimaced at the horror of it.

Suddenly, he felt his arms grabbed from behind. He squeezed his trigger, but the shot went awry. Then someone ripped the gun from his hand.

Unable to get a good look at his assailants, he struggled to free himself—but to no avail. As he was dragged to the base of the pyramid steps, he saw Freeze bring his weapon down and train it on him.

Clayton's heart was pounding in his chest, threatening to choke him. His legs were made of rubber. He swallowed hard, trying to find his voice.

"Please," he begged Mr. Freeze. "Have mercy . . ."

The figure in the silver suit descended slowly, majestically. He was shimmering, terrifying. And he seemed to like the idea.

"I'm afraid," he said, peering into Clayton's eyes, "that my condition has left me cold to your pleas."

Then, without warning, he fired his gun. A beam of energy shot out, engulfing the guard in its hideous, pale glow. He could feel every process in his body slowing down, going numb.

At long last, there was no disputing it. Clayton Krupzic definitely had ice water in his veins.

Freeze didn't let up on his cryonic beam until the guard was frozen solid. Then he reached out with his gloved fist and knocked on the man's icy cheek. The sound he heard was a hollow one.

"A copsicle," he observed.

His gang of thugs, whom he had dubbed the Icemen,

chuckled among themselves as they skated backward in their thermal suits. They were giving Freeze the space he craved—the space he deserved. He had trained them well, he mused.

Then he approached the shattered display case. With care not to puncture his suit, he began to wipe away the fragments of glass and steel.

"A brief lesson on the ways of the universe," he said to no one in particular. "Some substances are invulnerable to the heat of a thousand suns. There are stones that defy the weight of mountains piled on their backs. Certain sub-atomic particles exist forever and will outlive God himself. But in this universe," he pontificated, "there is only one absolute. Only one thing you can always depend on. Everything . . ."

He lifted a tremendous diamond from the debris of the display case. It sparkled magnificently in his hand.

". . . *freezes*," he said, completing his thought.

Freeze held the diamond high over his helmeted head. The light lanced through it, eliciting rainbows of color, making it shine more brilliantly than any star.

"From perfect beauty," he announced, "I will bring back . . . life."

Suddenly, the skylight seemed to explode, scattering daggers of glass that made the remains of the display case look like splinters. And in the wake of that unexpected explosion, Batman came plummeting into the room, his cape a huge, outflung shadow that darkened even the brilliance of the gem.

CHAPTER
2

Before Freeze could move a muscle, Batman hit the ice-covered brontosaurus and came sliding down its neck. Plowing into the villain feetfirst, the Dark Knight dislodged the diamond from his grasp and sent it skittering across the frozen floor.

Clenching his teeth, Freeze turned his cryonic weapon on his adversary. "Bat on ice, anyone?"

Abruptly, Batman kicked the cryo-gun out of Freeze's hands and snatched it out of the air. "Didn't your mother ever tell you not to play with guns?" he asked in that low, ominous voice of his.

Moving quickly, Freeze launched a kick of his own— and sent the gun pinwheeling out of Batman's possession. Then he snatched it in turn.

"You're not sending me to the cooler," he said.

Before Batman could respond, Freeze fired. But his enemy dodged the blast. Undaunted, Freeze took aim again.

That's when the front doors of the museum blew open—admitting Gotham's other costumed crime fighter. Robin came soaring through the air on his motorbike, a grin on his face as if there were nothing in the world he'd rather be doing than risking his life.

Freeze was so distracted by the entrance, he didn't see Batman kick at his gun again. He just felt the impact and saw the weapon ascend in a high, twirling arc.

At first, Freeze thought it was headed for Robin's hand. But Batman's protégé didn't catch it. Sailing over Freeze's head on his bike, he kicked the airborne gun onto the altar atop the pyramid.

"Score!" Robin laughed. "And the crowd goes wild!"

Then he landed, laying his bike sideways in a long, slippery slide across the floor. To keep from slamming into the wall, Robin grabbed a Roman statue of Mercury and used it to whip around in a dismount.

Batman went for Freeze. Robin was right behind him.

How dramatic, thought Freeze. *How inspiring.* His own outlook tended to be more down to earth. More succinct.

"Grab the gem," he told his Icemen. "Kill the heroes."

Until now, his hirelings had been holding back, awaiting his orders. Now they rushed forward, hockey masks in place, sticks flailing as they closed with the caped intruders.

"It's the hockey team from hell," Robin wisecracked.

He didn't know how right he was, Freeze mused, as he raced toward the altar and his fallen gun. But he never quite got there.

There was a rush of dark security uniforms from a side door Freeze hadn't paid much attention to. And before he could reach the top of the pyramid, they were swarming all over him.

It turned out to be a mistake. A *big* mistake—but not for Freeze.

After all, he was their superior in every way. A living weapon designed to survive, to endure, to *win*—while they were doughnut-chomping nobodies off the streets of Gotham.

With speed and precision, he began whaling on the guards. Hooks, jabs, upper and lower cuts—all perfectly delivered, if he did say so himself. And the inevitable result?

He looked at the uniformed figures sprawled all around him. Not a single one was still conscious.

"Cop-suey," he spat.

Then he remembered his gun, still atop the altar. Showing the rent-a-cops the disdain they deserved, he turned his back on them and went for it.

Batman blocked a swinging stick with his left hand, then kicked the offending Iceman in the ribs. Sensing danger from behind, he ducked and allowed a second Iceman to sail over his back. Then he punched the first one, sending him sprawling across the room.

A glance told him Robin was holding his own as well. But they weren't getting any closer to the giant gem the Icemen were defending.

Glancing at Freeze, Batman saw the villain ascending the pyramid, a string of guards littering the floor at its base. Clearly, the villain had to be the priority now.

Touching a stud on his belt, he popped a pair of skates out of the soles of his boots, took a couple of running steps to get up some momentum, and wove an intricate path through the Icemen.

En route, he bowled one over and grabbed his stick. Out of the corner of his eye, he saw that Robin had done the same. Together, they raced across the room on narrow steel blades, momentarily free of Freeze's henchmen, and headed for the pyramid.

But by then, Freeze had made it to his gun. Grasping it, he turned and fired, creating an ice bridge to the floor.

"Caution," he said, his voice devoid of inflection—and all the more sinister for it. "Bridge may ice over."

And with that, he slid down the ice bridge to the floor

below. Then he began sprinting toward his giant drilling truck.

Batman had to make a choice—and quickly. Freeze or the gem. He clapped Robin on the shoulder.

"You get the ice," he told his compatriot. "I'll get the Iceman."

"Gotcha," said Robin.

Batman didn't watch him make his way back through the maze of thugs—there was no time. But he did hear a series of grunts and curses that told him Robin was doing his job.

Now it was time for Batman to do his.

As Freeze raced for his truck, the Dark Knight was closing fast. Fast enough, perhaps, to prevent a clean getaway. Certainly, Freeze seemed to think so—because he spun around in mid-run and fired his cryo-gun.

Batman ducked, using his cape as an ice shield—and managed to deflect the beam toward one of the Icemen. The thug froze in his tracks.

Seeking cover, Freeze disappeared behind the giant brontosaurus. At the same time, Robin skated into line with Batman, both of them heading in the same direction.

With undisguised pride, the boy showed his mentor the diamond. "I got mine," he breathed. "Where's yours?"

Suddenly, the powerful-looking legs of the brontosaurus crusted over with a thick coat of ice. "What killed the dinosaurs?" bellowed Freeze, poking his head out from behind the brontosaurus. "Why, the Ice Age, of course."

Then Freeze shoved the beast with all his strength, causing the mighty creature to topple forward. As it hit the floor, it exploded in front of Batman and Robin.

"He's definitely extinct," Robin pointed out—always the master of the painfully obvious.

He and Batman managed to elude the debris, but had to veer off from their objective to do so. Unfortunately, it allowed the Icemen to catch up with them—and one of the henchmen took the opportunity to slash at Robin's hand. Again, the gem went tumbling free.

Another Iceman hit it with his stick. The diamond changed direction and went flying—toward a landing near the museum doors.

By that time, Freeze had made it to his truck. He was climbing forward to get to the hatch. And the Icemen had encircled the crime fighters, cutting them off from both the villain and the diamond.

Batman saw one chance. He skated straight at the thugs, pulling a flagpole from a display en route—as if he were planning to engage them in a joust. Picking up on his intent, Robin plucked a flagpole as well.

But at the last second, just as the Icemen braced themselves for the crime fighters' assault, Batman and Robin drove their poles into the ice-covered floor and vaulted over the Icemen's heads. As the thugs watched helplessly, the masked men flew through the air—in the direction of the landing and the waiting gem.

Before they could get there, Freeze yelled, "Hit me!"

Batman came to roost on the landing mere inches from the gem, Robin right behind him. But an Iceman skated in from the wings and, with a slapshot, sent the diamond flying across the room . . .

. . . right into Freeze's waiting glove. Batman saw the villain's fingers close over the gem, securing it.

"Thanks for playing!" Freeze crowed.

Then he dropped into the cockpit of his giant drilling truck and began to slide the hatch closed above him.

Batman turned to his protégé. "Work on the thugs," he said. "I'll take care of Freeze."

Before the words were out of his mouth, he saw a capsule rise out of the drill truck on some kind of ejection cylinder. He had to move quickly.

Leaping onto a banister that ran beside the landing, Batman retracted his skates. Then he slid down the rail on the soles of his boots and jumped when he got to the bottom.

For a heartbeat, he sailed through the air. Then he dropped into the cockpit. A fraction of a second later, the hatch closed over it.

Inside the capsule, Freeze was starting to feel the rush of victory. Making his way to his control console, he started to hit a button—when something dark and leathery caught his eye.

He whirled. And saw Batman standing there.

Of course. The fellow was nothing if not tenacious.

"Freeze," said the crime fighter.

Freeze smiled. "Nice of you to drop in."

Then he hit the button. A tremendous roar went up, and the capsule—set on the end of its ejection cylinder—blasted out of the drill truck. It rose like a rocket toward the roof.

Batman was thrown to the floor by the powerful acceleration. But Freeze remained upright, protected by his mighty suit.

"Pity the poor Bat," he said. "How weak you are."

As he made the comment, he saw something flash by one of his observation ports. A black-and-red blur that looked disgustingly like Batman's sidekick. And judging by the gloved fingers he saw clinging to the raised edge of the port, that was exactly who it was.

But he wouldn't be able to hang on long. Freeze was certain of that.

As if to underline his thought, the capsule blew through the ceiling at an angle, then blasted its way through the museum roof. They were suddenly surrounded by the starry night sky as the rocket continued to climb.

But Robin was still clinging to the side of the rocket for

dear life. Freeze grunted thoughtfully. Perhaps the junior crime fighter's demise would take longer than he'd imagined.

Batman glared at his adversary as he got to his feet. "You were a great scientist once, Freeze. A great man. Don't waste your genius on evil."

Freeze looked at him. "I hate being lectured," he said.

Then he shoved Batman into the bulkhead with bone-jarring force. And before his enemy could recover, the villain brought his cryo-gun to bear.

Pressing the trigger, he froze Batman's ankles and wrists to the bulkhead in chunks of dense, unbreakable ice.

Batman cursed himself inwardly. He had allowed Freeze to get the drop on him. And in a game like this one, it was difficult to come back from an early deficit.

"If I were you, I would watch the numbers," Freeze told him. He tapped his silver-gloved finger on the transparent face of the altimeter. "They are the harbingers of your doom."

Batman glanced at the altimeter. Their capsule was at ten thousand feet and climbing steadily.

"Can you feel it coming?" Freeze asked him, his voice as clinical as a scalpel, his eyes glazed with intellectual curiosity. "The embrace of the void? The icy cold of space?"

Batman didn't answer. He was thinking. There was a way out of this, if only he could find it.

"To freeze to death," his adversary went on. "What blissful agony. At ten thousand feet, a small quiver, a tiny quake. The body resists, thus far unaware that its fate is sealed."

Still, Batman refused to answer. In his mind, he was

entertaining strategy after strategy and rejecting them just as quickly.

"At twenty thousand feet," said Freeze, "the heavy hand of cold wraps you in a blanket. It slows your blood, chills your lungs. And then, at thirty thousand feet, what welcome relief. An end to rage, to pain, as your heart turns to ice and beats no more."

Another glance at the altimeter showed Batman they'd reached fifteen thousand feet. And still rising.

"In such a way," Freeze told him, "I was frozen once. In such a way I was torn from the warmth of human company. But fear not, my friend. You have imprinted yourself indelibly on the psyche of society. The world will not forget you as I was forgotten."

Freeze was distracted by something. Batman followed his gaze to one of the observation ports, but there was nothing to see.

Smiling coldly, Freeze turned back to him. "Your friend Robin was with us for a while," he said. "But he seems to have dropped off."

For a moment, Batman's heart sank in his chest. Then he caught a glimpse of a dark, slender figure outside the hull—hanging on to the capsule with the help of magnets on his hands and feet. Slowly but surely, his face showing the terrible strain, Robin was struggling against the acceleration—making his way inch by inch toward the escape hatch.

But Freeze couldn't see that from where he was standing. And Batman certainly wasn't about to tell him about it.

Besides, the villain was busy with something else. As Batman looked on, Freeze stepped into the straps of a glide-wing backpack mounted on the wall. And as if he were addressing a university physics class, he went on doggedly with his lecture.

"At forty thousand feet, the rocket's fuel will be exhausted. This icy tomb will plummet back to Gotham in the form of a fiery missile." Freeze gazed at Batman with something strangely akin to envy. "And you will live forever. In blessed infamy."

Batman scowled. "You're insane, Freeze. There are other ways to kill me, if that's what you're after. If this capsule lands in Gotham, it'll slaughter thousands of innocent people."

Freeze opened the door behind him, unleashing the fury of the dark and naked sky. The wind whipped at everything in the cabin.

"Innocent people get hurt all the time," he said with utter objectivity. "Freeze well, Batman."

And he leaped out into the night.

CHAPTER

3

For a moment, it felt to Freeze as if he were flying. Then gravity asserted its claim to him and he plummeted toward the lurid lights of Gotham City many thousands of feet below.

But it didn't worry him—not in the least. Calmly pressing a stud in his silver suit, Freeze watched as a sleek wing unfolded itself from his backpack. He felt it catch the wind.

Then, using body English, he angled himself downward in midair, using his glide wing to control his flight toward the Gotham skyline. As he descended, he contemplated a world without Batman.

Not bad, he thought. *Not bad at all.*

Batman strained against his icy bonds. Everything in the capsule was frosting over—the controls, the transparent nose cone, even the bulkheads. Just the way Freeze had expected.

But there was one thing he hadn't expected. As Batman

watched, the capsule's escape hatch opened and Robin lowered himself through it.

"I was just hanging around," Robin said, gathering his strength after his ordeal. "Thought I'd drop in."

Batman looked at him askance. "I thought you were going to stay in the museum and round up the thugs."

Robin's eyes widened in his mask. "You thought—?" he sputtered. "How about 'Nice to see you'? 'Glad you're here to save my life'?"

"That's not the point," Batman replied, "and you know it."

His companion didn't respond. Apparently, he didn't see any point in it. Instead, he pulled a laser from his Utility Belt and flash-melted one of Batman's ice shackles.

But Batman had no intention of dropping the matter. "When we get home," he said, "we're going to have a little interpersonal communication workshop. Just the two of us."

Robin sighed and flash-melted the other ice bonds, one at a time. Batman rubbed his wrists, finally free.

"So," said Robin, changing the subject, "is it kind of cold in here or is it just me?"

Batman glanced at the altimeter again. They were at twenty thousand feet and still ascending. Ice was forming everywhere. He imagined he could feel it stiffening his joints, thickening his blood.

But there was no time to dwell on that. He still had time to save the city—if he hurried.

"We've got to make sure this rocket doesn't turn Gotham into a crater," he said. He looked around and thought for a moment.

Then he whipped out a bat-shaped charge from his Utility Belt and threw it underhand at the ceiling, where it stuck fast. An armed light on the charge began to flash green.

"Now what?" asked Robin. "We call a taxi?"

Batman turned to one of the doors and gripped a handle marked CAUTION: EXPLOSIVE BOLTS. Divining his plan and apparently approving of it, Robin smiled and grabbed a similar handle on the opposing metal door.

"Watch the first step," Batman advised, keeping a straight face.

Robin nodded. "Surf's up."

Simultaneously, they pulled the release handles and leaped onto their respective capsule doors as the explosive bolts blew them into space. At the same time, the light on the Batcharge turned red.

As the wind whipped past him, Batman glanced at the capsule and counted to himself. When he reached "five," the capsule exploded above them in a thunderous, blood red flare.

Sizzling debris rained down on them. But he and his protégé managed to avoid it as they skyboarded downward on their capsule doors.

So much for making a crater out of Gotham, he thought. With luck, the remnants of the capsule would drift out to sea on the wind, where they wouldn't hurt a soul. But his work still wasn't done.

Below them, Freeze was zigzagging to earth, the diamond called the Second Sun of the Sudan in his hand. And to Batman's chagrin, he had a rather healthy head start.

Freeze wasn't expecting a sudden explosion in the starry heavens above Gotham. But as soon as he heard it, even before he looked up and saw its fiery aftermath, he knew what it meant.

He had underestimated Batman. *Again.*

And Robin as well, it seemed. Somehow, both the crime fighters had survived and were coming after him. On . . . he grunted appreciatively . . . on the doors of the obliterated capsule, of all things.

Still, Freeze wasn't perturbed. He still had his cryo-gun. And his wits. With both those very formidable weapons in his arsenal, he was confident he would yet carry the day.

It wouldn't be easy. It never was with those two. But in the end, Freeze would triumph.

Batman negotiated the wind currents with apparent abandon, his cape fluttering behind him, taking chances that might have been ill-advised under other circumstances. But unless he sped up the pace of his descent, he wouldn't have a prayer of catching up with Freeze—who had already dropped below the tops of the city's highest skyscrapers.

Robin was right with him, taking the same chances. But then, the boy had been a trapeze artist. His entire family had been comprised of trapeze artists. Working without a net was second nature to him.

The canyons of Gotham yawned. Lights flickered dizzily, impossibly distant but getting closer all the time.

Throwing his weight to the left, Batman avoided a turret as he plummeted after Freeze. Then he threw himself the other way to avoid the point of another building. Back and forth, down and down, closing the gap with each breathtaking twist and turn.

But would it be enough? Would they reach the villain in time to get the museum's diamond back? Batman gritted his teeth, knowing there was only one acceptable response to those questions.

One might as well have asked him if bats fly.

Slicing past an elevated bridge, Batman caught a quick glimpse of the motorists' faces as he dropped by, followed closely by Robin. They were astonished, to say the least.

Still far below, the streets of Gotham rushed up at the Dark Knight with increasing clarity and definition. And Freeze's lead wasn't diminishing quickly enough. Oh, he was looming closer and closer, but as long as Batman was at the mercy of the wind, he could descend only so quickly.

Coiling like the predator he was—the predator he *had* to be—Batman took the greatest chance of all. He leaped from his capsule door, relinquishing the only element of maneuverability he had, and fell through the night like a stone.

It was a calculated risk. If he wasn't knocked off course by a sudden gust of wind, if Freeze didn't see what he was doing and veer at the last moment, he would land directly on his objective.

But if Freeze *did* happen to look up—and elude the falling crime fighter—Batman didn't have a chance. At this rate of descent, there would be nothing he could do to save himself.

Another moment, Batman told himself. *Just one more . . .*

Indeed, Freeze turned to look back—but by then, it was too late. The Dark Knight hit him square in the glide pack and grabbed the villain around the neck. What's more, the impact knocked the diamond out of Freeze's hand.

As Batman hung on to his nemesis, gloved fingers clawing for purchase, he watched the gem tumble through the air. Even if he had his hands free, it was too far away for him to recover it. And if he didn't, it would shatter on the pavement below.

Fortunately, the hero's dilemma didn't last very long. A red-and-black figure swooped out of the night. Maneuvering in a grand flip, Robin snatched the falling gem.

The villain and the swag, both in hand. Batman was just beginning to look for a place to land when he saw Freeze reach down and release his glide-pack buckle.

Before Batman could respond, he found himself holding an empty glide pack. Freeze himself was dropping unassisted toward the giant, smoking chimney of a towering industrial complex.

Finger Foods, he thought. One of the bigger businesses in the city *not* owned by Wayne Enterprises.

Freeze aimed his cryo-gun at the smoking tower and fired. The maw of the chimney choked up instantly with snow—just a fraction of a second before the villain plummeted into it.

Once again, Batman felt he was in jeopardy of losing his prey. He flung Freeze's glide pack away and grabbed the limits of his cape. Then he arched his back and used the Kevlar of the cape like a rudder—to aim himself at the chimney headfirst.

His cape fluttering around his head like an entire swarm of bats, he sliced into the snowy opening. And caught a glimpse of Robin dropping in right after him, his capsule door discarded.

They found themselves dropping through one snowy layer after another in a madly snaking tunnel with walls of ice. Batman could see Freeze up ahead of them, firing as he fell, but nothing more.

Still, the chimney wouldn't go on forever. They had to break their fall before their fall broke them.

Pulling out his Batgrapple equipment, Batman made sure Robin saw what he was up to, then fired. Almost simultaneously, two grappling hooks hit the icy inner surface of the chimney and caught.

Gripping his tether with both hands, the Dark Knight managed to hang on as the line went taut—and nearly tore his arms out of their sockets. But a layer of ice, no matter how thick, just wasn't the ideal medium for a grappling hook. The sudden tug of his weight on the line jerked the Batgrapple free of the ice.

Batman fell, albeit not quite as quickly, into icy darkness. Somehow, he landed on his feet. Robin came to earth a heartbeat later. Then they heard the clatter of their grappling hooks hitting the ground.

They were in a long, submarinelike corridor. Or at least, that's what it looked like. Actually, Batman guessed, it was the basement of the Finger Foods complex.

Robin grinned at him in the murky light of an overhead bulb. "Cool," he said. "Can we do that again?"

Batman didn't bother to answer, and his protégé didn't bother to wait for one—because at the same moment they spotted Freeze at the far end of the corridor, trying to get away. As they took off after him, Batman saw him pause just long enough to point his gun at the ceiling and fire.

The pipes there—sprinkler pipes, apparently—exploded under the pressure of water expanding into ice. The result? An intense blizzard in the narrow confines of the corridor.

But that wasn't the worst of it, Batman knew. "Sudden temperature drop," he shouted. "Watch out for the—"

A blast of frigid air roared down the tunnel, slamming doors into walls ahead of them, beating them back with a powerful jolt of snow and ice.

"—wind!" Batman finished.

He and Robin whipped their capes over their windburned faces and pushed forward, fighting their way through the howling force of the storm. They went through the doors ahead of them one by one.

Finally, throwing open the last door in the tunnel, they burst into the boiler room. Of course, by then the place was frozen solid. A rime-covered boiler stood in the center of an icy moat that had, until recently, been the building's internal reservoir.

Obviously, Freeze had been here. But where was he now?

Suddenly, the heavy metal door slammed hard into Batman's face. He stumbled, dazed—but he had gotten the answer to his unspoken question. Freeze emerged from behind the door and aimed his gun at Batman.

But before he could fire, Robin interposed himself between Freeze and his target. His intent was no doubt to pounce on the villain, to take him down before he could injure Batman.

But it didn't quite work out that way.

Freeze fired—and Robin was enveloped in a point-blank blast of cryonic energy. One moment, he was a living, breathing human being—and the next, a frozen version of himself, openmouthed with shock.

The villain plucked the diamond from Robin's frigid hand.

But Batman was no longer quite so concerned about the gem. He wasn't concerned about anything except the frosted statue of his protégé.

He fought off horror. No, he told himself. It can't be. It couldn't end like this for Robin.

He wouldn't *let* it.

As he made that silent promise, Batman heard a rumbling in the ground and looked around. What . . . ?

And then he remembered. Freeze's drilling truck—they'd left it in the museum. And if it was anything like the Batmobile, Freeze could summon it via remote control. Batman imagined the thing burrowing its way underneath the city, freezing the rocks and dirt in its path and clearing away the debris as it zoned in on the boiler room.

Abruptly, with a shriek of bending metal and a crunch of concrete, a wall of the room exploded inward—and Batman didn't have to imagine the vehicle any longer. As the smoke cleared, the drilling truck loomed point first like some bizarre beast out of legend.

"How cold-blooded can you be?" Freeze asked his enemy. "You have eleven minutes to thaw the Bird before it's too late for him. What will you do—chase the villain or save the boy?"

A hatch opened in the giant vehicle, and Freeze leaped inside. But he didn't close the hatch just yet.

"Your emotions make you weak," he said. "Weak and vulnerable. That's why this day is mine."

And with that, Freeze shut the hatch. As he cleared the frosted pane of a window to say good-bye, the drilling truck withdrew into the ground. Before long, it had sealed the last part of its entry tunnel with a mighty blast of cryonic ice.

Batman had a bad taste in his mouth. He wasn't accustomed to letting criminals get away. But in this case, he'd had no choice.

Moving to Robin's side, he touched the boy's frozen skin. Eleven minutes—that's what Freeze had told him. But what if he was lying?

Batman knew he couldn't think that way. He had to do something before he lost his friend forever.

Whipping out his Bat-laser, he pointed it at the frozen reservoir and fired. The ice melted. It began to steam, to simmer.

Picking up Robin with the utmost care, the Dark Knight lowered the boy into the steaming liquid until he was completely immersed. But under the water, Robin's face was terribly still.

Deathly still.

For a long, heart-wrenching moment, Batman thought the boy was a goner. Then Robin's eyelids fluttered. A couple of bubbles broke the surface. There was movement, the sudden flapping of arms and legs.

Batman dragged the boy up until his head broke the surface. Robin coughed out water, took a wheezing, wet breath, and did it again. He looked weak, drained of energy.

But he was *alive*.

Then he clutched at Batman's arm and asked him something. But he was still gasping too hard to be understood.

"Say again?" Batman asked.

Robin looked up at him. "Did we . . . *get* him?"

The older man scowled beneath his mask. He didn't think his protégé was going to like the answer.

CHAPTER

4

Hoping for a breeze to relieve the dense, humid heat, Pamela Isley opened the door to one of her tents—more a soiled, smelly flap of canvas, really—just in time to see a jagged spike of lightning spasm in the darkness. Thunder followed, a deep, tremulous rumble that could be felt in her bones as well as heard.

But the storm notwithstanding, Pamela didn't find the breeze she'd hoped for. All she found was the same close, sweet-scented stillness, the same sticky, narcotizing stew she'd lived in for months now. The same monotonous drone of insect song.

In fact, the only change this night, besides the storm itself, was the number of vehicles braving the marshy road that wound its way through the rain forest—a road that ended in front of the half-ruined building against which her tent city was built.

What was the name of the place again? She could never remember, though she'd seen it every day. Oh yeah. Prison Morte. *Prison of Death.* Very colorful. Very funny. She was sure the inmates had laughed themselves silly.

The other thing it said on the building was "For Sale or Lease"—although she was pretty sure Dr. Woodrue wasn't paying any rent for his pile of rocks. Maybe it was another joke, she realized. A regular riot, this place.

It wasn't what she'd expected when she left Seattle, that was for darn sure. It wasn't even close.

Wiping the sweat from her brow, Pamela sighed, let the flap fall back into place, and made her way back to her stool. In the amber light of a flickering Bunsen burner, she inspected a beaker full of chemicals—one of many scattered around the tent.

The beaker was bubbling merrily. At least something was merry around here. Certainly, it wasn't *her.*

Pamela caught sight of herself in the metal of the burner, her precise features hidden by glasses and a frizz of bad hair, her shape obscured by her loosely fitting lab coat. *Lovely,* she thought sarcastically.

She had never been the cheerleader type. She'd accepted that long ago. But out here in the rain forest, her personal appearance was going from bad to absolutely terrible. Everywhere she looked, she had some kind of blemish, some interesting variety of rash.

Then again, what difference did it make? Who could she possibly impress? Dr. Woodrue? She chuckled despite herself. *Yeah, right.* She would sooner have swallowed a frog.

Assuming a more businesslike demeanor, she reached for her microrecorder, one of the few pieces of modern equipment Woodrue had allowed her. Clicking it on, she spoke into the metal cylinder.

"I still have high hopes for the animal-plant crossbreedings," she noted. "Despite the setbacks."

She surveyed two lab tables. One held a variety of plants she'd collected on her forays through the rain forest. The other was covered with tanks of poisonous spiders, snakes, and scorpions. Tubes ran from the lethal beasts into a jar of milky fluid labeled "Venom." More tubes ran from the Venom jar to the plants on the other table.

One plant twitched as it received the toxins. It was a good sign.

"If I can only find the correct dose of Venom," she said into the recorder, "these plants will be able to fight back like animals. I will have given flora a chance against the thoughtless . . ."

Her lip curled as she remembered.

Her mother's flower shop back in Seattle. The way those vandals had trashed it for a lark. The way they'd used their switchblades to cut and slash every living thing in it—every blessed shrub and perennial and houseplant.

And the way her mother had never gotten over it.

She could still smell the spilled-chlorophyll scent of death. The stomach-churning stench of rotting cellulose. The bitter taste of fear and helplessness . . .

". . . the thoughtless ravages of man," she finished.

Suddenly, she heard something. Not thunder. Something higher-pitched, but muffled. Some bird, maybe, screeching in the night? She listened, but the sound didn't repeat itself. She spoke again into her recorder.

"Where was I? Oh yes. On a more personal note, my work would proceed a lot faster if Dr. Woodrue weren't always whisking my Venom samples back to his mysterious Gilgamesh Wing."

She negotiated a path through the tents until she reached the old, massive-looking prison door to which the last tent was affixed. A sign referred to Woodrue's experiments, the ones conducted within the prison building, as Project Gilgamesh.

He had never explained what that meant. Nor had he showed her any of his work since she'd arrived.

"Why won't he let me into his lab?" she wondered out loud.

There was another scream—but this time, she was sure it hadn't come from any bird. It was too bloodcurdling. Too human.

And it had come from the other side of the prison door.

Cold sweat trickling down her back, Pamela turned off the recorder. "What is he doing in there?" she whispered.

Her mouth dry, her heart beating wildly, she came closer to the door. Put her ear to it. Listened for the scream.

Just then, the door opened. Pamela dropped her recorder as lightning flashed, illuminating Dr. Jason Woodrue, a man with Albert Einstein's hair and Charles Manson's eyes.

She'd always thought of him that way. But now, the comparisons took on a whole new significance.

"Dr. Isley," he said in his nasal voice, "loveliest flower in our garden. How fare our little wards?"

Before Pamela could reply, before she could force her heart back down her throat, Woodrue moved in too close for comfort. He backed her all the way to her worktable, his face mere inches from hers. Then his eyes fell on the jar of Venom in the farthest tent.

"What do we have here?" he inquired as he made his way through her equipment and supplies. "A lovely new supply of Venom?"

He reached the table, lifted the jar, and held it up for inspection. "I'll just take this to my laboratory for further study."

Pamela screwed up her courage. "What exactly are you working on in there?" she asked. "What are those screams I keep hearing?"

There was a bright flash of lightning. His face caught in its glare, Woodrue advanced on Pamela again.

"How I'd love to share my secrets with you," he told her. "But I ask you, sweet sapling, can you be trusted? You refuse my invitations to dine. You hide your honeyed buds behind these sallow robes."

He took the lapel of her lab coat between his spindly fingers. She pulled it away.

There was more lightning, followed by a deafening roll of thunder.

"Ah," whispered Woodrue, fashioning a toothy grin, "but there's romance in the air tonight. Perhaps a moonlit stroll in the jungle, eh? And then later, in the dark, we can share *everything*."

Abruptly, Woodrue backed her up against a table, his twitching lips only a finger's breadth from her own. Pamela winced, managed to sidestep him. Then she heard another scream.

"You have to tell me what you're doing with my Venom," she insisted.

Woodrue's features turned nasty. "You must show me your secrets, blossom, before I show you mine."

For a moment, Pamela thought he would attack her then and there. But he must have thought better of the notion, because he backed off. And, a moment later, turned and left.

As the door to the prison building swung closed, Pamela had an idea. She kicked her fallen recorder across the tent. The metal cylinder rolled between the prison door and the jamb, keeping the entrance from sealing.

And Woodrue didn't notice. Through the narrow opening, she could hear his footsteps retreating on the building's stone floor.

Pamela waited until she thought she had put enough time between her and Woodrue. Then, her pulse pounding in her temples, she took a deep breath and opened the door and followed the doctor inside.

She found herself in a crumbling hallway. There were no cells here, but the place had the smell of death about it. Death and pain.

As Pamela thought that, another scream split the air. But it was much louder now, with no door to shield her from it. Much louder and more heartrending. And it didn't stop there. There was another scream. And another, echoing through the corridor.

She followed them deeper into the prison. And deeper still. Finally, she felt as if she was almost on top of them.

Turning a corner, she peered into a large, dilapidated chamber that seemed like something out of a Frankenstein monster movie. That is, she told herself, with a few key updates.

Banks of overhead lights hung on long wires, suspended from the crumbling ceiling. A series of computers flashed tiny, red lights in repeating patterns. And in the center of the room, an empty gurney was surrounded by an array of circuits and tubes and equipment so arcane and so intricate, Pamela couldn't even *begin* to divine their function.

Woodrue walked past the doorway, showing himself to her without realizing it. He was speaking into a portable phone, nodding his strangely shaped head every few seconds. Finally, he looked up and addressed someone Pamela couldn't see. Curious, she crept closer to get a better view.

What she saw was a small bridge strung from one side of the room to the other. An American general, a high-ranking Russian officer, a sheikh, and the dictator of a Central American nation were all standing on the bridge, watching Woodrue from above.

Pamela couldn't believe it. She had thought the vehicles she'd seen arriving all evening were carrying supplies—not foreign dignitaries.

"Ladies and gentlemen of the un–United Nations," Woodrue began. Then he spoke deferentially into the phone. "And, of course, our mystery bidder. I give you the future of military conquest."

A scrawny prisoner in a too-large tank top was dragged into the room by several gun-toting guards. Pamela's eyes opened wide. Guards? Where had *they* come from? Had Woodrue had them in his employ all along?

As she watched, horrified, the prisoner was shackled to the gurney. His shaved head was adorned with three surgically implanted ducts.

"May I present Antonio Diego," said Woodrue. "Diego is a serial murderer who was serving a life sentence in an Argentine prison. He is also my sole surviving volunteer."

Diego glowered at the scientist. Without warning, the man spat.

"And what a charmer," Woodrue added.

That's when Pamela noticed a jar of milky Venom among the equipment hooked up to the gurney. Indignant, she slipped into the room, still unnoticed, and hid behind a stack of circuit boxes. If she was going to get the goods on him, she would need a ringside seat.

With his free hand, Woodrue lifted the jar of Venom so his guests could see it better. "The super-soldier serum," he announced proudly. "Code-named Venom. Patent pending, of course."

Then, slowly for the sake of drama, he put down the phone and poured the Venom into a high-tech injector strapped to the back of the gurney. Next, he held up an open-front black-and-white mask attached by snaking tubes to the injector pack.

"Notice the hassle-free zipper," he pointed out.

Pulling the oversize mask over Diego's head, he fit its tubes into the ducts in the murderer's skull. Finally, he zipped the fabric of the mask closed over the prisoner's face.

Taking a remote control device out of his pocket, Woodrue glanced at his audience. "Time to scream," he advised them cheerfully.

At the same time, he hit a control stud on the remote. The injector pack began pumping the milky Venom into Diego's skull. As Woodrue had promised, the man screamed.

And screamed.

And screamed.

But that wasn't the worst part. Something strange was happening to the prisoner right in front of Pamela's eyes. Something *hideous*.

His chest was beginning to enlarge noticeably. His neck was thickening, his forearms growing to massive proportions. There was a murmur of appreciation from the figures on the bridge.

Woodrue picked up the phone again. "Behold," he said. "That is, those of you who can. Muscle tissue volume and mass are actually increasing tenfold. But that's not even the tip of the iceberg. Venom stokes the fires of rage, fans the flames already inside a subject. In his current condition, Diego would kill to silence a grating voice . . . or darken the light in a pair of eyes that looked at him wrong."

The figures on the bridge took note. Clearly, they were impressed.

"The ideal killing machine," Woodrue went on. "I call this little number . . . Bane. As in 'bane of humanity.' Catchy, eh?"

His audience didn't respond to the scientist's remark. They were too intrigued by Bane himself.

Woodrue continued in the same high-pitched tone of excitement. "Imagine it, your own personal army made up of thousands of these super-soldiers. What force on earth could stand against you? Who would dare?"

He let that thought sink in for a moment. Then he held the phone up to his mouth, so whoever was on the other end couldn't miss his next remark. "The bidding begins at a mere ten million. Dollars, of course."

For good measure, Woodrue punched another stud on his remote and increased the Venom flow. Impossibly, the prisoner grew even larger.

His arm and leg shackles snapped. Sitting up and swinging his legs around, the monstrous Bane lurched for the

Venom pump, smashing equipment and computer consoles as he went.

One piece of equipment actually exploded, raining sparks down around Pamela. Closing her eyes, she shielded herself with her arms and waited a few moments. Then she looked up again.

To her utter dismay, Woodrue was hovering over her, his eyes more maniacal than ever. In the background, she could see the scientist's guards rushing to subdue Bane.

"Welcome to my parlor," said the scientist.

"I . . ." She tried to come up with an explanation, but it stuck in her throat. "You don't understand, I . . ."

"It's all right," Woodrue told her. "Really. All for the best."

Helping Pamela up, he escorted her back toward her lab. Still reeling from what she'd seen, she went willingly.

"You see," he told her en route, "our original sponsor had no stomach for military applications. He cut the funding for our work. In fact—"

"*Our* work?" she murmured. "I had nothing to do with that . . . that *creature* I saw in there."

Woodrue smiled. "But without your research, your Venom, I could never have come this far, my dear." His smile widened. "Join me, won't you, Pamela? The two of us entwined, side by side . . ."

He let his voice trail off suggestively.

By then, they had arrived at Pamela's tent—the one where she created the Venom. Woodrue opened the tent flap for her.

"Join you?" Pamela repeated, still numb from what she'd seen. She sat down on the nearest stool. "But I've spent my life trying to protect plants from extinction . . . and now you corrupt my research into some maniacal scheme for world domination."

She felt herself getting angry. She drew strength from it.

"When I get through with you," she told him, "you won't be able to get a job teaching high-school chemistry. You hear me, you grade-A psycho?"

Woodrue chewed the inside of his mouth. "Well," he said with eerie calm, "I can respect your opinion."

Then he shoved Pamela viciously backward into the interconnected tables. Plants and poisonous vermin came raining down on top of her as they spilled from their cages.

"Sadly," shrieked Woodrue, his eyes popping wildly, "I'm not very good at rejection!"

He began pulling down shelves full of cages and bubbling beakers. Their contents came crashing down on Pamela, burying her, burying all her specimens as well.

"I'm afraid you'll have to die!" he screamed at her.

He pulled down more equipment. More. Pamela felt herself crushed by the weight of it. She tried to struggle against that weight, but it was no use. She was overcome.

As blackness gathered before her eyes, she could see Woodrue grinning, taking pleasure in her death. She imagined him turning, heading back into the prison, where the bidding was about to start.

And she hated the idea. *Hated* it.

But not for long.

CHAPTER
5

Bruce Wayne stood by the main computer console in the Batcave and tapped in a command. Then he retreated a few steps to join his legal ward, Dick Grayson—who was wrapped in a heavy blanket, a steaming mug of hot cocoa in his hand.

"Gotham University Labs," said Bruce, eyeing the monitor. "Security video. Two years ago."

A moment later, an image sprang to life—that of a dazzling, high-tech laboratory. A beautiful young woman was lying on a gurney in the foreground as a lab-coated scientist worked on an elevated platform in the background, manipulating a bank of controls.

Below him, a vat of chemicals steamed and roiled. Bruce recognized the stuff as cryonic solution—a variation on which had made Dick a frozen statue in his guise as Robin.

Abruptly, the scientist looked up. It was Freeze—not as they had just seen him, but as a handsome, confident man at the top of his career. His eyes were warm and friendly, portals to a soul that seemed much the same.

"Dr. Victor Fries," said Bruce. "Two-time Olympian." He realized how that sounded and modified it. "Two-time

Olympic *decathlete*. Nobel Prize winner in molecular biology. After his wife, Nora, contracted a rare disease called McGregor's Syndrome, he hoped to freeze her in cryogenic sleep until he could discover a cure." Bruce frowned. "Watch closely. This is where everything goes north."

On the monitor screen, alarms began to sound. A panel exploded. And Fries, caught in the blast, was thrown into the vat of cryogenic solution.

"That liquid is fifty below," Bruce pointed out.

Bobbing to the surface, Fries screamed through the mists of the cryonic solution. His skin was frozen now, a bluish color. His hair was brittle where it still existed at all.

Dick winced in sympathy. "He's freezing alive. That's gotta hurt."

Fries was still bobbing. Still screaming in pain and terror.

"Somehow," Bruce said, "he survived. But the cryo-solution mutated his body. Made him something other than human."

The image on the monitor changed. It became a revolving schematic of Fries's unique physiology.

"What happened to his wife?" asked Dick.

Bruce remembered the woman he had seen that night on the athletic field. He remembered how beautiful she was.

He shrugged. "Presumed dead. No one knows."

The schematic turned into an image of Mr. Freeze. Then it outfitted him with his high-tech silver suit, layer by layer. When the computer was done, compartments in both of Freeze's sleeves were highlighted with flashing diamond shapes.

"He needs extreme cold to survive," Bruce went on. "His cryo-suit uses diamond-enhanced lasers to keep him at zero degrees."

Dick held up his hand. "Let me get this straight. A brilliant citizen, disfigured by a horrible accident, reemerges as a psychotic super-villain bent on theft, revenge, and destruction. You see a pattern here?"

Bruce returned Dick's somber expression. The boy was talking about Two-Face, of course—the district attorney turned master criminal who had shot Dick's parents to death.

The same paradigm seemed to fit the Riddler as well. And a number of other maniacs whom Batman had fought over the years.

"Maybe it's something in the water," Bruce replied.

He glanced thoughtfully at the screen again. "Well, if it's ice the Iceman wants . . ." He glanced over his shoulder at the costume vault, which stood at the far end of the cave. "Alfred?"

There was no answer. Bruce darted a glance at his ward. Dick shrugged. Bruce was about to see what was keeping his butler when Alfred emerged from the costume vault.

"Sorry, sir," he said. "The costumes needed more dusting than I thought. I lost track of the time. Did you require something?"

Bruce nodded. "The Wayne Diamonds, Alfred."

Dick jerked his head at the image of Freeze on the monitor. "We gonna trap ourselves a snowman?"

"Absolutely," said Bruce. He glanced at his ward. "Just as soon as you take ten hours training in the simulator."

Dick's mouth opened. Clearly, he'd been caught by surprise.

"Whoa," he said. "I made a mistake, I'm sorry. It won't happen again."

Bruce shook his head. "You were reckless," he insisted gently but firmly. "You could have been killed."

Dick held out his hands in an appeal for reason. "But I'm fine. See? I'm here, alive. How are we gonna work together, be a team, if you're never gonna trust me?"

"How indeed?" echoed Alfred.

Bruce was surprised by his butler's comment. He looked from Alfred to Dick and back again.

Then he smiled a wry smile. "When did *I* become the bad guy?"

Dick smiled back, but not as enthusiastically as he might have hoped. Alfred smiled, too, though more faintly.

Bruce cleared his throat. "Well, we've got to sleep sometime."

"Not me," Dick declined. "Not yet. I'm still too pumped."

Bruce nodded, understanding. "Suit yourself. Good night."

Dick nodded. "Good night." But his gaze had already strayed back to the monitor and its representation of Freeze.

Bruce headed for the winding stair that led from the Batcave into Wayne Manor. Alfred was right behind him. For a while, they walked in companionable silence. Then, when they were out of earshot of Dick, Bruce turned to his butler and close friend.

"You don't usually disagree with me," he noted.

"You were rather stern with him," Alfred observed.

"He's overeager," said Bruce. "He's impulsive. I can't trust him not to get himself hurt."

Alfred pondered the comment. "Perhaps the truth," he replied, "is that you don't really trust anyone."

Bruce frowned. "Don't tell me you're on his side."

His butler smiled benignly at him. "For all your talents, Master Bruce, you are still a novice in the ways of family. Master Dick follows the same star you do, but he arrives there by his own course. You must learn to trust. For that, I daresay, is the essence of family. *Trust.*"

They stepped through a doorway into the mansion's first-floor study, where a portrait of Bruce's parents hung over the fireplace. Alfred's quarters were just across the hall.

"I trust *you*," Bruce pointed out.

Alfred looked at him. He seemed oddly discomfited by his employer's words. "Thank you, sir. But I shan't be here forever."

Bruce returned the look. It wasn't like Alfred to express such sentiments. Then the butler smiled, dispelling Bruce's concern.

"Sleep well, sir," he said.

Bruce nodded. "You too, Alfred."

The butler repaired to his room for the night. Bruce stood there at the entrance to the study until he saw Alfred's door close. Then he turned away and looked down the hall . . .

. . . and saw himself come racing around the corner.

Not as an adult, but as a boy of no more than ten. As he watched, the youngster tripped and tumbled to the wooden floor. Immediately, another figure stepped past the corner to pick him up.

It was Alfred. A significantly younger Alfred. Kneeling beside the boy, he brushed off his knees and gave him comfort. He made it seem as if it didn't hurt at all.

Bruce blinked away the memory. Funny, he thought, that he should remember that just now. Then, undeniably fatigued from his escapades, he made his way down the empty hallway, its echoes loud in his ears as he sought the comfort of his bed.

Alfred closed the door of his bedroom and crossed the carpeted floor to his workstation. But as soon as he sat down, he felt the pain come back.

In waves. In pangs as sharp as kitchen knives. It was even worse than it had been in the costume vault, and that had been so bad he'd barely kept from crying out.

But as before, Alfred gritted his teeth and clenched his fists and endured what he had to endure. Finally, after what seemed like an eternity, the misery passed. He was drenched with perspiration.

However, Masters Bruce and Dick weren't the only ones with a modicum of determination in this household. Activating his computer, Alfred watched its screen light up. Then he lifted a compact disc from its holder, slipped it into his disc drive, and began to type.

An advisory came up on the screen in bright green letters. "Override engaged. Copying protected files."

Alfred lifted a microrecording unit and spoke into it. "Still unable to reach you," he said. "Have vital information you must see . . ."

One by one, the screen displayed the files he was copying. Batmobile schematics. Batsuit designs. Blueprints of the devices stored in Batman's Utility Belt.

All of Batman's secrets, kept since the night he took to the rooftops above Gotham. All of them essential to the continued effectiveness of Gotham's Dark Knight.

And all of them downloading to the compact disc.

Through a canopy of ivy, past the open flap of her tent, Pamela Isley could see a slice of sky. And the full moon that had risen over the roof of the Prison Morte complex.

But it didn't look the same as she remembered it— neither the sky nor the moon, nor Prison Morte itself. Everything was different. Everything had a certain glamour about it. A certain *glow*.

And she was different as well. She could feel it in her every cell. She was something she had never been before, something that in all likelihood had never existed before.

Hearing a voice, Pamela turned toward it. Focused on it.

It was Woodrue. He was hovering over her battery-powered laptop in the next tent, talking on his portable phone as he rifled through her research files.

"Yes, sir," he was saying. "I'm so pleased you won the bidding, your supreme . . . er, ruthlessness."

In the distance, someone screamed. Pamela remembered that he had a name now: *Bane*. As in the bane of humanity.

"We're making the final modifications on him right now," Woodrue was telling his high bidder. "We'll have a thousand super-soldiers out to you tomorrow by overnight mail . . ."

Ridiculous, she thought. *The man is insane.*

But even in the grip of his insanity, the scientist had accomplished his goal. Just as she would accomplish hers.

As Woodrue hung up, she began to move. To shrug off the ivy that enveloped her, concealed her. Noticing the disturbance, he turned to look at her.

She stood, casting off the jungle vines. As before, her reflection was cast back at her in one of her chemical beakers. But this time, it showed an altogether different personage.

Her hair was magenta. Her eyes were a chlorophyll green. And her ravaged clothes revealed the form and stature of a goddess.

Smiling, feeling a rather interesting change in her body chemistry, she approached Woodrue. He tilted his head with curiosity as he took in the sight of her.

"Dr. Isley?" he ventured. "Pamela? My God, you look great. I mean . . . for a dead woman."

Her smile deepened. "Hello, Jason. I can call you Jason, can't I? You know, I think I've had a change of heart."

Coming closer, she took him in her arms. He didn't resist, either. Slowly, languidly, she kissed him on the lips. Then she drew her face back to gaze into his eyes.

"Quite *literally* a change of heart," she added. "I don't think I'm human anymore, Jason. The animal-plant toxins had a rather unique effect on me." She thought it through as she spoke. "They replaced my blood with aloe, my skin with chlorophyll . . . and filled my lips with Venom."

Woodrue's brow furrowed beneath his wild shock of hair. "With Venom, you say? But that would mean . . ."

Suddenly, the man began to choke. He fell, clutching at his throat. Trying to speak or breathe and accomplishing neither.

"Silly me," she said, kneeling beside him. "I probably should have mentioned that I'm poison."

As she watched, Woodrue shivered and spasmed. But after a few moments, it stopped. He lay still, eyes fixed on eternity.

Pamela shrugged. "Oh well," she said. "It's a jungle in here."

Standing up, she turned to the beakers she had labored so long and hard over and—one by one—spilled their contents onto the floor. Then she picked up a Bunsen burner and threw it to the ground.

Its flame spilled out, latching on to the flammables in its vicinity. Before long, her lab was a conflagration, sending up tongues of fire and trails of black smoke.

"Let the flames touch the sky," she whispered. "The time has come for plants to take back the world so rightfully ours . . . for Nature to again assert her place in the scheme of things."

And she was Nature's agent, her spirit, her will. "I *am* Mother Nature," she declared. "And it's not nice to fool with me." She grinned, reveling in the blaze. "It's not nice at all."

As she left the tent, something caught Pamela's eye. She lifted a broken beaker. On it, there was a logo—that of Wayne Enterprises.

In the distance, she could hear Bane screaming his birth pain to the world. Bellowing like the biggest, baddest newborn anyone had ever imagined.

She turned in the direction of his cry. "Coming, Bane darling. After all, we've got a plane to catch, you and I."

CHAPTER

6

Freeze walked through the frozen bowels of his hideout, admiring the ice sculptures he had made. Subzero art, he thought appraisingly. He didn't care if it never caught on anywhere else. Here, in his lair, the sculptures made him feel at home.

Outside, this place was an abandoned ice-cream factory built in the shape of a snowman's face, a dripping cone stuck onto his frigid head. Inside, Freeze reflected with some satisfaction, it was an unbroken icescape. An arctic terrain that echoed the wasteland in his soul.

Up ahead of him, on what had once been the factory floor, Icemen and curvaceous Snow Bunnies in parkas ate frozen dinners, laughing at the wide-screen television they'd installed. One of the Bunnies separated herself from the others and approached him.

"Freezy," she said, batting her eyelashes at him, "I'm feeling kind of . . . hot."

Freeze grunted, not at all enamored of the name the woman had hung on him. "I find that unlikely," he told her.

"Okay," she conceded. "Truth is, I'm freezing. My hair is brittle, my skin is dry . . . but I don't care. I'd weather blizzards to have you. You're the most perfect man I've ever known."

Freeze scowled. "To be frozen. To never change. A life of perfect ice-olation." He shook his head. "There is no perfection in that."

The Bunny pressed herself against him. "Then let's turn up the heat," she purred suggestively.

Freeze glared at her from his Olympian height. "You are skating on thin ice," he said. "My passion thaws for one woman and one woman only."

She sighed alluringly. "Forget your frosty femme. These lips are wet and ready to get frostbitten."

Freeze dismissed her with a wave of his hand. "Hop away, little Bunny. Before I cool your jets. *Permanently*."

She recoiled at that—and well she might. His patience was limited, and everyone who worked for him knew it.

Muttering beneath her breath, the Bunny left him alone. He watched her go. It wasn't as if she didn't move him. He just couldn't allow himself to be disloyal to Nora—even if she *was* entombed in ice.

Freeze wondered how cold he could make his shower. He looked around for his aide-de-camp.

"Frosty!" he called.

The man was by his side before he knew it. "Yes, Boss?"

"Look at them," he said, indicating the Icemen and their Snow Bunnies with a tilt of his head. "Everyone is always having a good time—except me. Try as I might, I can find no pleasure in life. Perhaps my heart truly has turned to ice."

Suddenly, Freeze had an idea. He lifted his gun and fired, freezing Frosty into a solid block of ice.

The villain considered his work. "Well, that was fun," he commented grimly, ironically. "There's hope for me yet, I think."

Changing the setting on his gun, Freeze fired again. This

time, it emitted a thawing beam. Frosty seemed to come back to life, though he was soaked and dripping like a wet cat.

Without a word, Freeze turned and walked past his work area—and its mounting piles of scrawled schematics. He could hear Frosty following him.

"Tell me," Freeze said.

The response was almost instantaneous. "Anything, Mr. Freeze."

"Do you think I'm mad, Frosty?"

Frosty wrung out his sleeves. "That's really a judgment call, Boss. Not for me to say."

A soft beeping sound interrupted their conversation. Alerted by it, Freeze consulted his wrist display. The power gauge was on "low."

"Battling the Bat exhausted my power," he observed.

Freeze approached a safe. Opening it, he removed three small diamonds and placed them in his suit compartment. Immediately, his power levels spiked back to normal.

"But I was successful nevertheless," he added.

Freeze continued to a pedestal, atop which sat a machine powered by two giant diamonds. There were slots for two more diamonds, still empty. Smiling to himself, he reached into his tunic and removed the diamond stolen from the Gotham Museum. Then he placed it in one of the empty slots.

"One more giant diamond of this size," he told Frosty. "One more and my freezing cannon will be complete. I will hold Gotham ransom. Unless the city bows to my demands, it's winter forever here in goat-town."

"The city fathers will cough up millions," said Frosty, coughing even at the thought of it.

"Billions," Freeze corrected. "They'll have no choice." He turned to gaze at a frozen wall. "Then I'll have the funds I need to complete my research. To find the cure for . . ."

His eyes narrowed as he continued to stare at the wall. As he thought about what—and who—was on the other side of it.

"Leave us," he said abruptly. "We need quality time."

Frosty complied. As soon as his aide had slunk out of sight, Freeze opened a door in the wall and entered a walk-in freezer. There, he found a frozen-dinner box and lifted it—causing a door like that found on a bank vault to swing open.

Lifting his chin, he stepped into what looked like a frozen mausoleum. In the center of it stood a computerized, glacial sarcophagus with a transparent face. He walked up to it and bent over to get a better look.

Inside it, he could see his frozen wife, ineffably beautiful in near death, a snowflake pendant gracing her frigid breast. Lovingly, he touched the transparent material separating them.

Memories came to him. Of better times. Of life and warmth. Unfortunately, they were only memories, encased as she was in a casket of ice.

"Soon," he promised, "we will be together once more."

Then, reluctantly, he straightened and took his leave of her. After all, he couldn't revive her without curing the disease that had taken her.

And so far, he hadn't even come close.

Dick was emerging from the Batcave, still sweaty after a rigorous training session, when he heard the doorbell ring.

His first impulse was to get the door. After all, he hadn't grown up in a mansion with servants catering to him all the time. He'd spent most of his youth around circus people, who did for themselves.

But in the short time he'd been living here, he'd learned

that Alfred got the door. Just Alfred, no one else. That was the protocol.

So he stopped himself. And waited for Alfred to get it.

The doorbell rang a second time. *Now, that's unusual,* Dick told himself. Emerging from the study, he followed the hallway past the stairwell and into the foyer.

Squinting at the light that streamed in from the half-circle window above the door, Dick looked around—and saw Bruce coming from the direction of the dining room, obviously with the same question on his lips.

"Where's Alfred?" they asked simultaneously.

The bell rang a third time.

Suddenly, Alfred appeared behind them. "I must have dozed off," the butler explained—and not without a certain amount of embarrassment. As he confronted Bruce, he looked painfully contrite. "My sincerest apologies, sir."

Bruce held up a hand and smiled. "First time in thirty years, Alfred. I think we can find it in our hearts to overlook it."

Dick looked at the door. The suspense was killing him. Wayne Manor didn't get too many visitors, mostly since Bruce didn't encourage them. So he couldn't wait to find out who was there.

Without further ado, he opened the door. "Mystery pizza delivery?" he wondered out loud.

A beautiful young woman stood before him, her blond hair catching the golden autumn light. She was dressed in prim, schoolgirl clothes.

Dick swallowed. "Please be looking for me," he said. Inwardly, he added another *please*.

The girl smiled. "I'm sorry to trouble you, but—"

Her eyes drifted from Dick to Bruce and beyond. It was then that they lit up like beacons.

"Uncle Alfred?" she exclaimed.

Suddenly, she rushed past Dick and Bruce and leaped

into the butler's arms. Alfred held her to him with obvious affection—and obvious surprise.

And he wasn't the only one.

Dick looked at Bruce. Bruce shrugged. Together, they mouthed the word "uncle?"

Barbara Wilson felt as if she were in a fairy tale as her hosts gave her the Grand Tour of Wayne Manor.

Only in her dreams had she seen anyplace like it. It was so big, so stately, so majestic it almost didn't seem real.

The garden was especially magnificent, taking advantage as it did of the brightest and most vivid autumn hues. As she strolled through it, Barbara felt an impulse to take her "uncle's" arm in her own.

"The wisteria bushes are marvelous," she observed. "Fantastic color. Quite a surprise so late in the year."

Alfred grunted softly in agreement. "As are you, my dear."

Barbara laughed. "More of a shock, I suspect. How long has it been since we saw each other last?"

"Since my last visit to England?" The butler thought for a moment. "Two years," he concluded.

"Two years, three months, four days," she said. "Roughly."

Alfred turned to his employer. "Barbara isn't really my niece, sir. She's Margaret Clark's daughter."

Bruce nodded. "Of course." He seemed to regard Barbara with new respect. Or was it merely curiosity? "You know, Alfred still keeps your mother's photograph in his room."

Dick cleared his throat. "Anybody want to tell us kids in the cheap seats who Margaret Clark is?"

Alfred turned to Dick. "Ah, yes. I don't suppose you would know that, would you?" He paused reflectively.

"Margaret and I fell in love while I was visiting Metropolis a very long time ago. But when I realized the difference in our ages was unfair to her . . ."

Barbara finished the sentence. "Uncle Alfred returned to Gotham. Much to Mother's dismay, I might add."

"Eventually," said Alfred, "she married a young physician. I wouldn't imagine she was unhappy with the turn of events."

"Alfred's main squeeze," Dick remarked devilishly, as they approached the stables. "Is she here?"

The young woman felt herself reddening. Her "uncle" was blushing as well, she noticed.

"Don't tell me," Dick sighed. "I'm about to scrape the bottom of my shoe off my tongue."

Recovering, Barbara smiled sympathetically. "My parents were killed in an auto accident ten years ago. Alfred has been supporting me ever since."

Bruce seemed surprised. "You have?" he asked.

The butler shrugged. "Secrets *are* a virtual prerequisite in this house, don't you think?"

Barbara didn't understand the reference. But then, every family had its little quirks. As friendly as this one appeared, she was sure it was no exception to the rule.

"At any rate," she said, "I'm on break from—"

"Oxbridge Academy," Bruce said. "Alfred's alma mater."

She looked at him. "Their new computer sciences division, yes. But how on earth did you know that?"

"I recognized the accent," he told her.

She looked at him askance. "The . . . accent?" As far as she could tell, she hadn't picked one up.

"All right," Bruce conceded, a youngster caught with his hand in the proverbial cookie jar. He pointed to a school crest on her sweater. "It says so on your patch."

Barbara rolled her eyes. "I should have known."

By then, they had come to the garage. An ebony-colored

motorcycle stood out front. Barbara couldn't help grinning at the sight of it. It was so streamlined, so rich-looking as it caught the sunlight.

"What is it?" she asked, coming close enough to run her fingers along its chassis. "It's beautiful."

"You can say that again," Dick muttered.

Barbara turned to him—and saw he wasn't looking at the motorcycle. He was looking at *her*.

She tried not to giggle as he waxed serious to conceal his embarrassment.

"It's, er, a competition racer I've been fixing up," he said. "A vintage Black Knight. Maybe one day I'll show you how to ride."

"You most certainly will *not*," Alfred interjected.

"Thank you anyway," said Barbara, waving away the suggestion, "but to be honest, those things frighten me."

"Well," Bruce remarked, "riding lessons or not, I hope you'll stay with us while you're here in the States."

"Actually," said Alfred, "there's a lovely inn just down the—"

"All this luxury really isn't my style," the young woman confessed, hoping her interruption didn't seem rude to her uncle. "But . . ." She eyed the bike. "The truth is I'd actually *love* to stay."

"Then it's settled," Bruce declared hospitably.

Alfred frowned. "Oh, but, sir, so much goes on—"

"Don't be silly," Bruce told him. "After all, Alfred, she's family."

Barbara smiled. She was family, all right—though not *his*.

Pamela Isley—or rather, the woman who had *been* Pamela Isley—stood in the lee of the plane from which she had just disembarked, on the starlit tarmac of Gotham

Airport. She was dressed all in black, her newly unique coloration obscured by a widow's veil.

Luggage handlers scurried all around her. She watched them remove an immense black coffin from the plane's cargo hold.

"Be careful," Pamela said. "He's always been a little touchy."

The foreman grunted with the magnitude of his effort. "Right. Whatever you say, lady."

She overheard him speak to one of his fellow handlers as they wrestled the coffin onto their truck.

"What did she feed this guy? *Lead*?"

"He's always been touchy," echoed the other handler. "Uh-huh. Like he's gonna sit up and complain about it."

Suddenly, a giant fist came crashing through the coffin lid, splintering it into fragments. And in its wake, a hulking, leather-clad form emerged. A rather terrifying apparition under the circumstances, Pamela imagined.

It was Bane, of course, in full costume, his Venom-injector pack strapped to his back. As Pamela looked on through her veil, he waded in among the baggage handlers.

"Geez Louise!" cried one of them, backing off in fear, his eyes as wide as airplane wheels.

But he wasn't quick enough to elude Bane. Reaching out, the giant grabbed him and began swinging him like a baseball bat, sending the other handlers flying in every direction. Every time he made contact, there was a thud of bone hitting bone.

Pamela smiled. She had never realized how satisfying a little death and destruction could be.

CHAPTER

7

As he dressed for bed, Alfred glanced at the photograph on the other side of the room. It stood there in a wooden frame in a place of honor on his dresser, just as it had every day and night for more than three decades.

Crossing the room, he picked it up and gazed at it and remembered. Oh, the things he remembered.

The insistence with which the rain had begun pounding on the wide, gray streets of Metropolis, hissing like an angry serpent. The remarkable scarcity of taxicabs just minutes after the downpour began. The way he'd spotted one and made for it like a bandit.

As luck would have it, a young lady had arrived at the cab door at the same time as he. And her eyes—so dark, so expressive—had looked up into his. Without thinking, Alfred had suggested they share the ride. Perhaps with just as little thought, spurred by the inclemency of the weather, she had agreed to the proposition.

It was only afterward that they'd discussed their respective destinations. He had been headed for the city's premier department store, she for the theater—where she enjoyed a minor part in a popular musical.

"Oh?" he'd said. "My mother was an actress. In fact, I dabbled in the West End establishments once myself."

Her delight in that discovery had led to an invitation. A ticket for the evening's performance, impossible to come by otherwise. And just like that, their two destinations had become one, the prospect of visiting Dacy's no longer quite so tempting to him.

After the performance was over, he'd told her how much he enjoyed her contribution, small as it was. It had been no more than the truth. She had potential, it had seemed to his practiced eye. And if she remained there in Metropolis, with its abundance of high-profile productions, it had a chance of being realized.

After that it was dinner for two at Balducci's, where the waiters were kind enough to give them a secluded table, though they must have wondered what such a lovely young woman saw in a middle-aged gentleman like himself. And they'd talked of this and that, though words were hardly the only things that passed between them.

Why hadn't he remained in the theater? she wondered.

He spoke of his father and his father's father, manservants through and through, and the footsteps in which he had eventually followed. And he spoke of his employers, the Waynes, though she hadn't heard of them.

He had smiled and assured her that she *would* have heard of them, if she had lived in Gotham rather than Metropolis.

Eventually, even their very patient hosts had expressed a desire to go home. Alfred had imagined that the evening, wonderful as it was, had come to an end.

But it was not so.

Taking his hand, Margaret had led him across town in the direction of the West River. And there he had glimpsed a strange and wondrous structure looming on the riverbank. A gaudy contraption of yellow-painted metal.

A tram support, of all things. As they got closer, he had seen its twin on the opposite shore. And between them, yellow cable cars trundling in either direction, reflected in the swirling currents of the river.

Long before they set foot in their private cable car and swung out high into the clean, clear night, long before he looked down into the dark, glistening water or peered ahead at the lights of Queensland Park . . . before all that, Alfred knew he had fallen in love with her.

What was worse, she had seemed to know it. And worse still, she had fallen for him with equal intensity.

He should never have let it go that far. He knew that even then. But he had. And *she* had. And despite the way things had turned out, he refused to regret one incandescent moment of it.

With a deep sigh, Alfred replaced the photograph on his dresser and turned to his workstation. He was tempted to use it as he had used it the last several nights. But he was too tired, too hollowed out from his ordeals during the day.

Better to go to sleep, he told himself, and start fresh in the morning.

There were four limousines waiting in line when Pamela Isley approached the airport's brightly lit passenger terminal. One limo was too small, another too old and clunky. Of the two more attractive ones, one was black and the other was navy blue.

She went for the black one. After all, it was a more natural accoutrement to her outfit.

As she walked around to the passenger's door, she saw the driver sitting inside, reading a nudie magazine. He didn't seem to notice her.

Pamela opened the door and slipped into the backseat. That got the driver's attention. In fact, his eyes opened wide at the sight of her. But then, he'd probably never seen a widow like her before.

"Hey," he said, "I was supposed to pick up a *guy*. No one said anything about a dame . . . I mean a *lady*."

She slid aside the partition between herself and the driver. Then she beckoned to him with her silken, black-gloved finger.

"Come here," she told him.

"Where?" he asked warily.

"Right here," she said, leaning forward on the seat until her face was framed in the opening. She smiled suggestively.

The driver hesitated for a moment. Then he chuckled and turned around in his seat. His nostrils flared, drinking in what he must have thought was some exotic and expensive perfume.

"Okay," he said, "what is it?"

"Don't look now," she whispered provocatively, "but I think you're about to be replaced."

The man looked at her quizzically. "Huh?"

Suddenly, a hand reached in through the open window—a *huge* hand—and snapped the driver's neck. Then his door opened, and he was dragged out onto the pavement.

A moment later, Bane inserted his huge bulk behind the driver's wheel. He was about to put the engine in gear when the door beside Pamela opened again—and a man in a business suit slid in.

"Boy, it was nuts back there," he groaned. "There was some kind of fight out on the tarmac and—"

He stopped as soon as he caught sight of Pamela. Reddening noticeably, he looked around.

"I'm sorry," he said weakly. "There must be some mistake—"

Pamela smiled. "Silly darling, there's no need to pretend in front of the driver." Grabbing his face, she kissed him passionately.

By the time she let go, the man was dead. As he slumped to the floor, Pamela reached over and opened the door. Then she pushed him out with her foot. He slid to the ground beside the limo driver.

"Love hurts," she advised the corpses as she closed the door. "In my case, it kills."

Bane glanced back at her over his massive shoulder. There was a question implicit in his bestial, bloodshot eyes.

Pamela thought for a moment. "Once around the park," she instructed him. "Then we'll see."

As she explored the ground floor of elegant Wayne Manor, her long terry-cloth robe sweeping the floor, Barbara Wilson saw that Uncle Alfred's door was ajar. Approaching it, she knocked softly.

No answer.

Making her way inside, she saw that the room was empty. A computer monitor and keyboard sat on her uncle's desk. Beside them, there was a neat stack of light blue airmail envelopes.

A closer look showed her they were all addressed to Wilfred Pennyworth at the Royal Court of Mirajanpore. And every one of them, it seemed, was stamped RETURN TO SENDER.

Suddenly, Barbara heard the sound of someone clearing his throat. Startled, she whirled . . .

. . . and saw her uncle standing half in shadow, dressed in his robe. He stepped out into the light. "I didn't know sneaking around was part of the curriculum at Oxbridge."

"I'm sorry," she said, blushing. "I came to tuck you in and . . ."

Alfred grunted softly. "*You* came to tuck *me* in. That's a switch."

He glanced at the envelopes on the desk and sighed. "As you can see, I am looking for my brother, Wilfred.

He is first butler to the Maharajah of Mirajanpore. But Mirajanpore is a floating court—it travels across India. So Wilfred can be rather difficult to find."

Alfred tapped the keyboard of his computer. The screen suddenly came alive with full-motion images of a resplendent royal court, carried entirely on the backs of elephants.

"I guess they don't have fax machines on pachyderms," Barbara observed.

Alfred chuckled wearily. "I have been trying to reach Wilfred with no success. As one grows older, you see, one yearns for family."

Barbara glanced at a framed photo on her uncle's dresser. A woman's face bore the inscription: *All My Love, Peg.*

The girl knew the face rather well. It was her mother's. In fact, she had that same picture by her bed at home. But . . .

"Peg?" she asked.

"My nickname for sweet Margaret," Alfred explained. "The heart often finds its own language."

Barbara smiled at his romanticism. "It's good to see you again, Uncle. I've missed you."

"As I've missed you," said Alfred. He embraced her and kissed her forehead. "Sleep well, child."

Barbara left his room, closing the door behind her. She waited for the light under her uncle's door to go out. Once it did that, she walked back in the direction of the stairs and her own room.

It was fun walking through the old mansion, ascending the grand staircase and negotiating the well-appointed hallway on the second floor. Like having some big antique hotel all to oneself.

But not half as much fun as what she intended.

Entering her bedroom, Barbara closed the door behind her—then whipped off her robe. Underneath, she was wearing a tight black leather motorcycle outfit. Moving to the far side of her bed, she retrieved a pair of sleek black boots and pulled them on.

Next, she removed a knotted climbing rope from her bags and tied one end of it to the post of her heavy, wooden bed—just as she had done so many times back at school. Then she slung a backpack over her shoulder and dropped the other end of the rope out the window.

Barbara descended in the moonlight as noiselessly as possible. Once on the ground, she avoided the mansion's lights as she made her way across the yard and headed for the Wayne garage.

Fortunately, it wasn't locked. The door wasn't even closed.

Inside the garage, she moved stealthily in the shadows, past the ridiculously expensive sports cars and limousines. At last, she came to the row of motorcycles she'd seen earlier in the day.

Stopping alongside Dick's sleek competition bike, Barbara climbed on and pulled a racing helmet from her backpack. Then she expertly kick-started the engine and rode out through the open doorway into the night.

Freeze's henchmen were either asleep or out on the town. He didn't really care which. Right now, he had more important things on his mind.

Standing at his workstation, he entered new data into his computer. A new approach he'd only just thought of.

"Maybe this time," he said to no one who could hear him. "Maybe *this* one will return you to me."

Holding his breath, he hit the key that sent the test program into action. In the bowels of his computer, nucleotide variations were created and applied at breakneck speed, accomplishing in theory what it would've taken months and years for a researcher to do in fact.

Freeze waited, hoping one of the variations would be the antigen he sought. After little more than a minute, he got his answer.

An alert panel flashed a simple message: TEST FAILURE. Freeze slammed the console with his fist.

Then he rose and walked through the open door to the vault where his wife still lay in her sarcophagus. Unchanged.

Once, Freeze would have cried for her. Now he couldn't even do that.

"No cure tonight," he whispered. "Forgive me, my love. But soon, I promise you. Soon . . ."

It was morning in Gotham City.

Bane was driving. Pamela was sitting in the backseat of the limo they'd boosted the night before. She was inserting brown contact lenses and donning a dark wig. Once more, she looked like Pamela Isley.

As she considered herself in a flip-down mirror, she sang a little song to the tune of a popular perfume jingle. "Kind of hip, kind of wow, Ivy. Kind of free, kind of now, Iveeee . . ."

When the stone-and-copper edifice of Gotham Observatory came in sight, Pamela showed Bane where she wanted him to pull over. Then she glanced again at the newspaper lying on the seat beside her. It was open to an article about the observatory's restoration.

The limo stopped a couple of blocks from the building, which was built on the banks of the broad, blue Gotham River. "I'll walk from here," she told Bane, then got out and proceeded on foot.

It took only a couple of minutes to enter the building and find the press conference mentioned in the paper. The conference was being held in an immense circular hall that appeared to be still very much under construction. A huge telescope was partially installed.

On a raised platform at one end of the hall, in front of a bank of blank television monitors, stood the immensely rich and powerful Bruce Wayne. He was flanked by his stunningly beautiful date and two men who looked like scientists. In this case, astronomers.

Pamela knew the type. After all, she'd been a scientist herself until recent events made her so much more.

She was much more intrigued by the billionaire industrialist than by his companions. Wayne seldom showed his undeniably handsome face in public. That made this a rare occasion—and a rare opportunity for *her*.

She cared least of all about the sexpot on the stage— though she recognized her as well. Julie Madison, screen celebrity and one of the hottest names in Hollywood— though some said her star had risen only because of her association with the mysterious Mr. Wayne.

The press was seated in front of the platform. Pamela joined them.

"My father," said Wayne, who apparently was just beginning his speech, "was a wise man. A man of compassion and accomplishment. He told me once that to succeed, we need only pick our star and follow it. And so Wayne Enterprises is donating the world's most advanced telescope to Gotham City's Observatory Restoration Project. Perhaps this telescope will give future generations a chance to find their own stars."

One of the journalists stood up. Pamela recognized her as Gossip Gerty of *Good Morning Gotham,* one of those morning talk shows.

"Bruce," she asked, "is it true this new telescope can see all around the world?"

One of the scientists answered her question. "Yes, it is. If you'll watch the monitors . . ."

Suddenly, the screens behind him came alive with a graphic of the earth. Several satellites were highlighted, all of them the same distance from one another and from the globe.

"Satellites already in orbit allow us to reflect light around the planet," the scientist went on.

On each monitor, a graphic ray of light was reflected from a satellite over Australia to a satellite over the United States—and then beamed to a graphic of the Gotham-based telescope.

"From here," said the other scientist, "we'll be able to see the sky anywhere on earth."

"Just don't point it at my bedroom," said the woman beside Bruce Wayne. Her remark got a laugh.

Gossip Gerty stood up again. "Bruce, you and the exquisite Julie Madison have been going out for what seems like forever. Are you planning to tie the knot?"

Wayne flushed. "Get married? Me? No . . ."

"*No?*" echoed the lovely Miss Madison.

Her wealthy date looked flustered. "Um, what I mean is . . . we have no plans at the moment . . ."

"But soon," said Julie, flashing her perfect teeth.

"Soon?" asked Gerty, no doubt hoping for some more dirt.

Wayne tugged on his collar. "Ah . . . soon*er* or later . . . all relationships evolve and . . ."

"And?" asked Gerty.

The billionaire turned to his companion. "Can I get some help over here?"

Julie smiled and turned to the press, the very picture of composure. "Bruce and I are lucky enough to be reck-lessly in love. And that is most certainly enough for us." She turned to Wayne and added, in a voice that was barely audible, "for now."

The press laughed, charmed by her wit. Pamela just rolled her eyes. If this kept up, she'd lose her lunch.

"Now," said the first scientist, "if you'll all follow me, I'll show you the central control grid . . ."

Leading the press to the telescope, the scientist continued speaking about it. His associate and Miss Madison followed as well.

But not Bruce Wayne. He stayed by the platform to confer with two of his aides. Seeing her chance, Pamela jumped on it.

But before she could reach the megamogul, a guard stopped her. "Sorry, miss. I don't see a press pass."

"Yes," she said reasonably. "I'm aware of that. But I need to speak with Mr. Wayne."

The guard shook his head. "No can do."

"But it's very important," she insisted.

Suddenly, Wayne's head turned in their direction. A moment later, he came over and addressed the guard.

"What's going on, Ted?" he asked softly.

The guard frowned at Pamela. "She doesn't have a pass, sir."

Wayne smiled and waved the guard off. "It's all right."

"If you're sure, sir . . ."

"I'm sure," the industrialist said. He turned to Pamela. "You're not going to hurt me, are you, Miss . . . ?"

"*Doctor*," Pamela corrected. "Doctor Pamela Isley."

Wayne looked apologetic. "Doctor, then. What can I do for you? If you're looking for a research grant, I'm afraid I'm the wrong one to talk to. But I can tell you whom to contact at the Wayne Foundation . . ."

She looked at him, undaunted. "Actually, I already work for you. Or did. Your arboreal preservation project in South America."

He thought for a moment. "Oh, yes. But . . . I believe we cut our support for that. A conflict of ideologies, you understand. To put it bluntly, Dr. Woodrue was a lunatic."

"I see you knew him," Pamela observed.

Wayne's eyes narrowed. "As I recall, that lab was consumed by fire last week. How did you manage to escape?"

Pamela ignored the question. Instead, she handed him a document she'd made up on her way to the press conference.

"I have here a proposal," she said, "showing how Wayne Enterprises can immediately cease all actions that toxify our environment."

Wayne took the proposal, opened it up, and scanned it. His brow furrowed as he read.

"Forget the stars," she told him. "Look here, at the earth, our mother, our womb. She deserves our loyalty and protection. And yet you spoil her lands, poison her oceans, blacken her skies. You're killing her."

The industrialist looked up, apparently having read enough. He appeared sympathetic to her cause. For a brief moment, she had a feeling he might go along with her plan.

Then she sensed resistance in him. Hostility. She girded herself for the inevitable combat.

"Your intentions are noble," Wayne conceded. "But with no diesel fuel for heat, no coolants to preserve food . . . millions of people would die of cold and hunger alone."

Pamela shrugged. "Acceptable losses in a battle to save the planet."

He raised an eyebrow. "I disagree. I've always believed people come first, Doctor Isley."

By then, the crowd of media types had returned. They were all in a tizzy about the telescope. *Fools,* Pamela thought.

Frustrated, she turned to them. "Mammals!"

They looked at her with varying degrees of surprise and curiosity.

"I beg your pardon?" said a distinguished-looking television reporter.

"You're so smug in your towers of stone and glass," Pamela went on. "So ignorant of Mother Earth and her ways, so blind. A day of reckoning is coming. The same plants and flowers that saw you crawl from the primordial soup will reclaim this planet.

"Earth will be a garden again," she told them. "Somehow, I will find a way to bring your man-made civilization to its knees. And there will be no one to protect you. *No* one."

She expected consternation, even fear. What she got was laughter.

"You must be new in town," replied Gossip Gerty. "In Gotham City, Batman and Robin protect us. Even from plants and flowers." Her eyes twinkled as she turned to Bruce Wayne. "Speaking of which . . . will the delicious Miss Madison be your date tonight at the Gotham Botanical Gardens?"

The billionaire cleared his throat. "You mean the Flower Ball, of course."

"Of course," Gerty confirmed.

It was as if they'd forgotten about Pamela and her warning. Dismissed her like some annoying little bug.

"Well," said Wayne, "although my foundation is hosting the event, I regret I'll be unable to attend. But I trust the rest of you will enjoy yourselves. Thank you all for coming."

He turned to Pamela. "Good day, Doctor."

She grabbed him by the sleeve, unable to contain her anger any longer. "Tell me," she rasped. "Would you warm faster to my pleas if I looked more like Miss January here?" With a jerk of her head, she indicated the lovely Julie Madison.

Wayne didn't answer. He just took his arm back and moved away, trailed by the press. Pamela glared at him.

Suddenly, she had an idea. Maybe she'd just picked the wrong event to crash—and also the wrong way to crash it.

But she'd rectify that error soon enough.

CHAPTER

Freeze remembered it as if it were yesterday.

As he watched, Victor Fries and his wife Nora turned to one another on their wedding altar. Looked into each other's eyes. And kissed.

It was a deep, passionate kiss, much to the embarrassment of the presiding clergyman. But they didn't care. They were in love.

Abruptly, the scene switched. Fries and his wife were playing with a puppy in a field somewhere. Upstate New York, he thought—or was it New Hampshire? It was the height of summer, judging by the brightness of the light and the cut of their clothes.

What was the dog's name again? He thought for a moment. Sunshine? Sunspot? Something like that. It was getting harder and harder for Freeze to remember such things.

His old self got up and left the video frame for a moment, grinning like a Cheshire cat. When he came back, he was still grinning. He handed Nora something. A long, slender jewelry box.

Her eyes grew wide as she opened it. "Oh, Victor," she said, "it's beautiful. I can't believe you—"

At a loss for words, she held the contents up for the

camera. It was a snowflake necklace, made of platinum and diamonds—the same one she wore in her icy tomb.

Nora placed the chain around her neck, closed her eyes, and basked in the warm, summer sun. It glinted in her hair, striking highlights. The dog leaped suddenly into her lap, probably wondering why she'd stopped paying attention to it.

In the video, Victor Fries put his arms around his wife. "Beautiful," he agreed. "But not half as beautiful as you are."

What's more, he still thought that. Still believed it with all the soul he had left. Even in her frozen state, Nora was the most beautiful creature he had ever seen.

" 'Scuse me, Chief."

Freeze turned and saw Frosty standing behind him. As usual, his aide looked tentative, apologetic.

"I didn't mean to interrupt," said Frosty, "but I got something here you might want to see."

He held out a newspaper clipping.

Without a word, Freeze lifted his gun and fired. In a flash, Frosty had frozen solid, still grasping the clipping.

"I hate it when people talk during the movie," he muttered.

Then he turned back to the video screen. He and Nora were on a sailboat now. A white sailboat on a painfully blue sea. The wind was in her hair and she was laughing, and he could see the snowflake pendant sparkle in the hollow at the base of her throat.

His lip began to quiver ever so slightly. It wasn't fair, he told himself. It wasn't fair at all. For someone so lovely and full of energy to be stricken with such a disease . . .

Suddenly, Freeze couldn't take it anymore. Lifting his cryo-gun, he aimed it at the screen and fired. The sailing trip exploded into a hundred flying shards of light.

He whispered to the smoking, sparking ruin of the monitor. "One more diamond, my love. One more."

Freeze got up and began to walk away. Then he noticed the newspaper clipping in Frosty's frozen hand. Breaking the paper off, he read it.

It said Bruce Wayne, the filthy-rich philanthropist, was donating a diamond to the Flower Ball that evening. Nodding, Freeze crumpled the paper in his gloved hand.

A *diamond*, he thought. How convenient. He could almost taste his wife's lips again beneath his own.

Inside the Gotham Botanical Gardens, an immense glass greenhouse set atop the roof of a mighty skyscraper, a hanging banner that read GOTHAM CHARITY FLOWER BALL blotted out the stars overhead. A giant beast mask covered the entrance to the place, so every guest who entered had to do so through the beast's mouth.

Drummers were pounding on conga drums, and all the guests were dressed as flowers—all except two, that is. And those two were dressed as gorillas who romped and cavorted about the room as if they were real.

But the guests weren't the only ones in disguise, Batman reflected. He himself was dressed as an employee of the gardens in a loose, brown jumpsuit. The same for Robin. And each was wearing a disguise that would have stood up even to the closest scrutiny, thanks to Alfred's well-earned cunning at theatrical makeup.

As a publicity ploy, the Flower Ball had invited Batman and Robin to attend the party through an ad in the *Gotham Gazette*. But of course, they hadn't responded to the invitation.

Batman didn't like to show himself in public places, preferring to remain a creature of uncertain reality—an urban legend of sorts. If he was never pinned down, never defined, that legend could continue to grow. It could insinuate itself into the dark heart of the city.

So when he confronted a bunch of hoods in a lonely alley, it wasn't a man they faced. It was whatever they imagined him to be—and that was usually far more terrifying than anything he could become in truth.

Still, Batman couldn't have avoided the ball entirely. Not if he hoped to close the trap he'd laid as Bruce Wayne.

"You think Freeze will take the bait?" asked Robin, sotto voce.

"He'll be here," Batman asserted. "He won't be able to resist."

Up on the stage, the president of the Gotham Botanical Club came out alongside the infamous Gossip Gerty. "Ladies and gentlemen," he said, "Gerty and I would like to welcome you to the gem of our evening."

Heeding their cue, two armed guards emerged from behind a curtain bearing a cushioned velvet pallet. In the center of the pallet, suspended from a silver chain, lay a perfect, grapefruit-size diamond.

The crowd murmured its admiration for the gem. But Batman paid no attention to it. He was looking around, checking the crowd, wondering when Freeze would make his move.

"The famed Heart of Isis," said Gerty, "on loan from the collection of my close personal friend, Bruce Wayne."

The president of the Botanical Club gestured gracefully and several women stepped forward, all dressed as flowers. Each one was more strikingly beautiful than her predecessor.

"Tonight," he said, "on auction, an opportunity to dine with one of our fabulous flowers—the famed diamond draped around her neck."

"Ooo," said Gerty, "look at all these luscious lovelies. Let's start the bidding, shall we?"

A man in the audience called out, "Ten thousand for Chrysanthemum."

"Twenty thousand for Lilac," yelled another.

"Thirty thousand for Rose."

But Gerty wasn't impressed, apparently. "Come on, boys," she roared at them. "Show some gusto!"

At the top of the stairs, one of the two gorillas was beating the drums all of a sudden. Batman's jaw clenched. Where were the drummers?

As he pondered the question, the other gorilla began to remove her costume. First, her paws. Then the gorilla head. And so on.

Until a vision of loveliness stepped out. of the costume—a creature more beautiful than any Batman had seen before or was likely to see again. She was wearing a skintight costume that appeared to be made of leaves.

Green boots and mask. Magenta hair . . . ? And the greenest eyes one could imagine. So green, in fact, they seemed to glow.

"Gorilla my dreams," Robin sighed.

The woman in green lifted her gloved hands, each one filled with a pile of sparkling dust, and blew it over the startled attendees. With agonizing slowness, the dust spun out in intricate fairy-tale spirals, curling its way through the crowd.

A moment later, everyone seemed spellbound, mesmerized. Languidly, she leaned back—and fell. But her fall was broken by the arms of several jungle-clad men on the ballroom floor.

As if on command, the men knelt—and she sauntered over a bridge made of their backs, through the parting crowd, toward the stage. The president of the Botanical Club looked on as she approached, openmouthed with awe.

"Hi, there," said the woman, lifting the man's chin with a slender forefinger. She winked at him.

"And, er, you are . . . ?" he sputtered.

"Poison," she said, smiling. "Poison Ivy."

Poison Ivy, Batman thought, trying to focus on her features. But it wasn't easy. He felt like a man who had drunk a quart of love potion.

Like everyone else, he had been swept up in a rush of devotion for the woman he could neither shake nor comprehend. If she'd asked him to swim an ocean for her, it would've been difficult to refuse.

Placing her hand on the club president's shoulder, Ivy gently pushed him into the background. "I'll take it from here," she told him.

Lifting the diamond, she put its chain around her neck. And no one stopped her. Not the audience, not the security guards . . . and not Batman. He was too fascinated with her beauty to move an inch, much less want to.

"Why bid for something as cold as ice when you can have a hothouse flower instead?" she asked. "Some lucky boy is going to hit the honey pot tonight. Whoever bids highest gets an evening of my precious company. I'll bring everything you see here . . . plus everything you don't. And most important of all," she added seductively, "I'll bring my imagination."

The offer started a riot of responses. "Fifty thousand for Poison Ivy," called one man.

"One hundred thousand for Poison Ivy," cried another.

"One million," shouted a third man. It took a moment for Batman to realize it was *him*.

Robin looked at him. In horror, thought the Dark Knight. His sidekick was no doubt aghast that Batman had joined in the bidding, caught up helplessly in Ivy's spell.

Then, to Batman's shock and dismay, the disguised Robin raised his voice as well. "*Two* million!" he yelled.

Batman whispered, "You don't *have* two million." Then, at the top of his lungs, he bid: "*Three* million!"

"I'll borrow it from you," the younger man told him. "*Four* million!"

"From the janitors!" Ivy laughed, obviously entertained

by the notion. "You two boys aren't going to fight over little old me, are you?"

Batman glowered at Robin. He felt like an animal, fighting over the most desirable female in the pack. But he couldn't help it. He wanted Ivy. *Needed* Ivy. And he would do anything to get her.

Then, out of nowhere, Gossip Gerty made a face and asked, "Is it me, or is it getting nippy in here?"

Suddenly, the teeth of the giant mask at the entrance exploded into fragments as a huge drill truck came smashing into the room—no doubt from an elevated bridge outside. There was no question about to whom the vehicle belonged. Freeze himself was standing atop the truck, backed dramatically by swirling mists, with his Icemen following close behind.

With a flourish, he drew his gun. "Did I use the wrong door *again*?" he bellowed.

Batman didn't know what brought him out of his lovestruck stupor—whether it was the abrupt drop in temperature or the triggering of instincts he'd honed since his parents' deaths. Nor, at this point, did he have much time to figure it out.

Stripping off his janitor jumpsuit, which had been held together with Velcro, he reached into his Utility Belt for his Batarang. Before even he was aware of it, his reflexes took over and the thing was slicing through the air.

Freeze never saw it coming. It knocked his cryo-weapon out of his hand.

A moment later, Robin was revealed as well. And like Batman, he seemed to be free of Ivy's enchantment. Together, they raced forward—

—and were engulfed in an opposing tide of Icemen.

Batman saw Freeze's weapon land in the hands of an innocent guest. As the man tried to determine what to do with it, one of Freeze's thugs rammed the guest from behind. The pistol went flying end over end.

By then, the Botanical Gardens' security guards had boiled onto the scene. With an appropriate sense of urgency, they swamped Freeze.

"When technology fails," the villain had time to shout, "resort to simple brute force!"

And with that as a battle cry, Freeze went into action. Moving with blinding speed for such a big man, he smashed guard after guard and whipped them into the midst of the frightened guests.

In the meantime, his pistol bounced from one person to another, guest to henchman and back again like a wildly fumbled football. Finally, a thug tipped the soaring gun back to Freeze.

And there was nothing Batman could do to prevent it. He was too busy trading blows with the Icemen.

Out of the corner of his eye, he saw the villain reach up and catch his hurtling weapon. "All right," he roared. "Everyone . . . *chill*!"

But of course, no one did. They were too scared, too confused. So Freeze fired at them, turning several guests and more than a few exotic flower arrangements into ice sculptures.

Freeze considered his handiwork and grunted appreciatively. "I should've been a decorator," he said. Then he started for the stage.

Across the room, Batman and his sidekick seemed to have their hands full with Freeze's Icemen. As Freeze watched, Batman smashed one thug in the mouth while Robin felled another with a spinning sidekick. Then he ducked, sending a second Iceman crashing into a third.

Freeze made a clicking sound with his tongue. Good help was hard to find, he mused, and climbed onto the stage—to face the woman in green who seemed to be running the show.

He didn't know who she was, but she was wearing the diamond he wanted. That made her an object of great interest to him.

"Let me guess," he said haughtily, dispassionately. "Plant Girl? Vine Lady? Miss Moss?"

The woman scowled. "Listen, Captain Cold. The suit, maybe, even though silver went out with the seventies. But those boots are unforgivable. What is it with you men, anyway?"

Freeze glanced at his adversaries. Slowly but surely, they were fighting their way toward the stage.

"I'd love to stand here all day and exchange fashion tips, but I'm pressed for time. So hand over the diamond, Garden Gal." He pointed his weapon at her for emphasis. "Or I'll turn you into mulch."

The woman didn't do what he asked. Instead, she reached into her belt pouch, pulled out a handful of dust, and blew it in his face. The dust swirled around his helmet—a result that seemed to perplex her.

"Pheromone dust," he guessed. "Designed to heat a man's blood—but it doesn't work on the coldhearted." He held out his gloved hand. "Now, if you please, the diamond . . ."

The woman sighed. "Well, if you insist," she said. She handed over the priceless gem.

He nodded. "Clever little clover."

Just then, one of Freeze's men flew across the room, smashing into the back of the stage. He noticed.

"That's my exit cue," he told the woman.

And before she could react, he was racing for his drill truck.

Poison Ivy watched the man called Freeze leap into his vehicle. She had never seen anyone quite like him.

So good-looking, in a grotesque sort of way. So masculine. So fabulously . . . she sought the right word.

Elemental.

And she was something of an elemental herself, now wasn't she?

A moment later, Batman and Robin—the self-proclaimed Gotham Guardians—raced after Freeze. But they didn't stand a chance against Freeze and his men. At least, she hoped they didn't.

Abruptly, Ivy realized there was something in her hand. A souvenir, left there by Mr. Freeze. A tiny glass globe that said *Welcome to Gotham*. She shook the bauble and saw the tiny city within caught in the throes of an all-consuming blizzard.

"Eleven minutes to thaw them!" someone shouted. "That's what Batman said, boys!"

Ivy turned and saw Police Commissioner Gordon standing near her. Normally, the commissioner was tough as nails, the glue that held the police force together. Or anyway, that's what she had heard.

Right now, he was looking at her the way a man might be expected to look at the most beautiful woman he'd ever seen—no matter how levelheaded he was at other times. Almost shyly, the commissioner pushed his glasses back on his nose and approached her.

His eyes were drawn to the globe in her hand. "What's that?" he asked.

She shrugged. "A gift from Mr. Freeze."

Gordon's demeanor turned a notch more serious. A notch more solicitous of her welfare. "Miss Ivy," he said, "you've just met one of the most sinister men in Gotham."

She gazed into the globe, where fake snow was piling up in great drifts. "That's no man," she breathed. "That's a god."

Gordon probably hadn't heard her—and even if he had, he had more pressing matters to attend to. He moved off as Ivy's fellow gorilla arrived on stage and removed his hot, stifling mask.

It was Bane, of course.

"Enough monkey business," she told her henchman, glancing at the globe again despite herself. "We've got work to do."

CHAPTER

By the time Batman reached his Batmobile and Robin leaped onto his Redbird, Mr. Freeze had eked out a significant head start.

But to paraphrase a certain ex-ballplayer, it wasn't over until the fat lady sang. And Batman wasn't hearing any warbling just yet.

Perhaps half a mile up ahead, knifing its way through the darkness, Freeze's drill truck led two similar vehicles over one of the interconnecting bridges that crisscrossed Gotham's skyline. Gothamites veered their cars off the roadway ahead of the villain, desperate to get out of his way, but so far there hadn't been any accidents.

Still, Freeze had to stay well below maximum speed to keep from swerving off the road himself, and his escape route would have been thoroughly planned. That meant he had something in mind.

A moment later, Batman found out what it was. A giant freeze gun atop the drill truck fired—and hit a massive statue looming ahead of it. Instantly, there was an explosion in the statue's neck, creating a storm of ice and a hole big enough to drive a truck through—

—which was exactly what Freeze seemed to have in mind.

Leaping off the road, the villain drove through the hole and raced onto the statue's shoulder. His cronies followed him as he made a beeline down the statue's arm.

Gritting his teeth, Batman accelerated and blew through the gap in the statue's neck as well. In the process, he glanced back at Robin in his sideview mirror. From the seat of his Redbird, Robin gave him a thumbs-up, full of confidence.

Then he followed the Batmobile through. Batman scowled. This kind of surface was chancy enough with four wheels. But with two . . .

Up ahead, Freeze's convoy was closing in on the statue's hand. Batman hit a button in the Batmobile's control console and a series of schematics lit up. They showed him the various trajectories of Freeze's vehicles and their imminent jumps from the hand, over the abyss of the city, to the lower rooftops of Gotham beyond.

Batman peered at Robin again and tilted his head forward, activating the radio hidden in his cowl.

"Pull back," he said. "You can't make the jump."

The wind whipping in his face, Robin shook his head. "I *can*."

The Batmobile shot down the statue's arm, the Redbird close behind.

"Pull back," Batman repeated.

"I can make it," Robin insisted.

Abruptly, he shot a wheelie, overtaking the Batmobile.

Batman looked to one of the monitors built into his dashboard. "Redbird control codes," he said out loud.

A moment later, the schematics for the Redbird flashed on the monitor.

"Disable engine," said Batman.

He saw the Redbird's engine warning light begin to flash. His protégé reacted with frustration as his motor began to die. Still, the abyss was coming up fast. The boy would have to accept his situation before he went over the brink.

Batman bit his lip. He'd had a choice to make and he'd made it—for Robin's own good. Now he could only hope.

Fortunately, his sidekick's bike-riding skills hadn't deserted him. As Batman looked on, Robin side-grounded the Redbird, skidding viciously but slowing down nonetheless.

At the same time, Freeze and his cronies split toward separate fingers of the statue. Their superthrusters fired, and Freeze's drill truck made the jump, heading for a sloping roof on the other side of the abyss.

His henchmen's trucks followed, flying into the air toward the rooftops beyond. But Batman could see they hadn't achieved the required height. Their trajectories wouldn't carry them as far as Freeze's had.

There was a moment when their occupants must have realized that. When the cold fingers of Death must have closed around their hearts, eager to claim the rest of them.

Then the suspense was over. One truck crashed through an elevated billboard, doomed to destroy itself on the streets below. The other smashed into a building and exploded in a red-orange burst of flames.

Only Freeze's vehicle made it to safety, hitting the sloped roof with brakes screeching. Spinning 180 degrees, it came to a stop with its freeze gun pointing back the way it had come.

Pointing toward its pursuers, Batman thought. *How convenient.*

The Redbird, meanwhile, was sliding dangerously close to the end of the statue's finger and the urban abyss below. But Robin finally wrestled it to a halt . . . just as Batman slammed his vehicle into top gear and roared past his protégé.

The Batmobile left the finger like a rocket and flew over the chasm. In his rearview mirror, Batman could see Robin standing on the statue's fingertip, shouting his rage into the night. But he could deal with that later. Right now, he had to have his wits about him.

As the Batmobile soared over the abyss toward Freeze's truck, its freeze gun fired a deadly barrage. Catching the Batmobile in midflight, the cryonic blast began to ice it over.

Batman cursed inwardly as he saw his controls had frozen solid. A monitor flashed, alerting him to widespread systems failure. And the windshield was piling up with ice.

The Batmobile was falling through the night like a frozen sculpture. Batman had to do something. Gritting his teeth, he reached for one of the few controls that still might work.

Pressing a button, he braced himself.

Abruptly, his windshield exploded and he was catapulted through the cloud of icy shards like a torpedo. He flew into the air high above the dark, spire-studded city.

He was pleased to see the Batmobile drop to the safety of the rooftops on the other side of the abyss. But now, it was his own safety about which he was most concerned.

Executing a flip, he whipped his cape open like the wings of a giant, dark angel and angled down, riding the night winds in a racing glide toward Freeze's truck below.

Fortunately, his cape had a lightweight metal framework, the kind that allowed him to swoop through the sky when the conditions were right.

He could see his shadow fall over the truck's open cab. Freeze had to be seeing it, too. But there was no time for him to do anything about it.

Batman smashed into him, knocking his helmeted face into the steering wheel with bone-crushing force. As Freeze's head snapped back again, the crime fighter grabbed him by the scruff of his suit.

Then—still airborne—he wrenched Freeze out of the

cab and spread his wings as a brake against the wind. A moment later, he landed in the moonlight, allowing a stunned Freeze to slump to the ground—the diamond still in his silver-gloved hand.

There was no fight left in the villain. No impulse to resist. It had all been knocked out of him.

"I'm putting you on ice," Batman told him.

And he was nothing if not a man of his word.

Bruce watched his young friend pace the length of the Batcave. Dick was red-faced, furious.

"I could have made that jump," he insisted.

"You could have splattered your brains on the side of the building," Bruce explained—yet again—trying his best to be patient.

After all, he'd been there. He knew what it was like to hurt inside. To want to set things right all at once. To want to turn unimaginable horror into someone's salvation.

"You know," Dick went on, "in the circus, the Flying Graysons were a team. We had to depend on each other. Each of us had to trust the others to do their parts, or we were finished. That's what being partners is all about. Sometimes, the only way to win is by counting on some-one else."

Bruce smiled tautly. "Be reasonable. You couldn't even keep your mind on the job at hand. All you could think about was Poison Ivy."

Dick exploded—at least partly, Bruce thought, because the older man had hit the nail on the head. "I was *doing* the job at hand," he snapped. "And as far as Poison Ivy goes, I wasn't the only one—"

"—smitten by her. I know," Bruce conceded, refusing to let the conversation devolve into tit for tat. "But there's a difference. Whatever happened at the Flower Ball, I was able to put it out of my mind. I was able to focus. Obviously, you couldn't do that."

The younger man's mouth became a thin, hard line. "Is that your *interpretation* of it?"

Careful. "That's the way I saw it, yes."

"Uh-huh. And the way you saw it is the way it happened, right?" Dick shook his head derisively. "Always, every time, the world according to Bruce. That's your idea of friendship, too. Your view, your house, your rules. Your way or the highway." The boy's muscles worked in his jaw. "And you know what? I'm sick of it!"

Bruce felt something tighten within him. Still, he kept his voice even, controlled. "Yes," he said, "they're my rules. But they keep us alive. And if you want to stay on this team, you'll have to abide by them."

Suddenly, Dick was right in his face. "Of all the pig-headed—!"

Whatever he was going to say after that, he must have thought better of it—because he stopped himself and took a breath. And another.

"This is no partnership," Dick rasped, his voice calm now but hollow. "You're *never* going to trust me, are you?"

Then he turned and stalked off.

Bruce watched him go. The boy would cool off, he told himself. He would see things in the light of reason.

But even as he thought it, he wasn't so sure.

As Bruce approached Alfred's room, he could hear someone talking inside. The last thing he wanted to do was eavesdrop. Clearing his throat, he knocked on the butler's door.

A moment later, Alfred answered it. "Won't you come in?" he asked.

"Thank you," said Bruce.

The television was on in the background. Hence, the talking he had heard from the hallway.

The screen showed the billionaire's alter ego fighting his way toward Freeze at the Flower Ball. He didn't know where the video camera had come from, but fortunately it hadn't gotten a good shot of Batman.

Alfred looked at him. "Congratulations on your apprehension of Mr. Freeze, sir. Batman rather monopolized the evening news."

Bruce nodded. "Thanks." But he didn't feel especially celebratory at that particular moment.

What's more, his friend and confidant picked up on it. "Is there something wrong, sir?"

The billionaire sighed. "Alfred, am I . . ." He recalled the words Dick had spoken in anger, still feeling the sting of them. "Am I . . . pigheaded? Is it always my way or the highway?"

The butler thought about it. "Why, yes," he replied at last. "Now that you mention it, it is very much that way."

Bruce wasn't sure what kind of answer he'd expected, but that wasn't it. "It is?" he asked again.

"Indubitably, sir." Obviously, Alfred had given this some thought. "You see, death and chance stole your parents. But rather than become a victim, you have done everything in your power to control the fates. To stack the deck in your favor. For what is Batman if not an effort to master the chaos that sweeps our world? An attempt to control everything—including the specter of Death itself?"

Bruce gazed out the window, into the darkness. He imagined that he saw two figures out there under an umbrella, laying wreaths on a rainswept grave. Himself, as a boy of course, and Alfred. As the adult Bruce watched, the butler put his arm around the boy and held him close.

"But I can't do it, can I?" he asked, returning to the here and now. "I can't control death."

It was a rhetorical question, but Alfred confirmed it anyway. "No, sir. I'm afraid none of us can."

And yet, thought Bruce, determination stiffening in him like an old habit, *how can I not continue to* try?

Still smoldering with anger and resentment, Dick went out to the garage. It was where he felt most at home—the one place at Wayne Manor that was more his than Bruce's.

But even as he entered and reveled in the sight of all those gorgeous machines, he couldn't help hearing Bruce's words in his head. Couldn't help remembering the sting of them.

"They're my rules."

And what was that business about Poison Ivy? Sure, there had been a moment there when he had been entranced by her—just like everyone else in the room. But the moment had passed.

By the time he had kicked the Redbird into gear up on that statue, Ivy was a memory. He had known exactly what he was doing when he gunned the engine to make the leap after Freeze's drill truck.

". . . my rules."

Who did Bruce think he was? Dick's *father*?

Not by a long shot. John Grayson had died at the hands of Two-Face, along with Dick's mother and brother Chris. They were gone, all of them, and no one could replace them.

". . . my rules."

Besides, he wasn't a baby anymore. He didn't need a nursemaid. Didn't need anyone telling him what to—

Suddenly, he heard the scrape of footsteps in the darkness. His training taking over, he crouched and looked for the source of them.

Dick caught sight of a shadow moving among other shadows. Someone was wheeling a bike across the floor of the garage. Someone slender and . . .

It was Barbara, their houseguest.

But what was she doing here? Where was she taking the motorcycle?

Only one way to find out, he told himself. Approaching Barbara from behind, Dick tapped her on the shoulder. Lightly, so she wouldn't be alarmed.

Suddenly, he felt himself flying through the air, the victim of a well-executed judo move. Rough landing, too.

Dick could've handled it better if he had been even the least bit prepared for it—but, of course, he wasn't. After all, it wasn't Bruce Lee he'd tapped on the shoulder. It was only Alfred's prim, proper niece from some stuffy English boarding school.

Barbara looked down at him, horrified. "Oh, I'm so sorry," she gasped. "So dreadfully sorry."

"Uh, right," he said, rubbing his elbow where it had slammed into the concrete of the garage floor. But it was his pride that hurt more.

She glanced contritely at the bike she'd wheeled in— Dick's high-performance number. "I'd just never seen anything quite like it, you understand. Anything so . . . I don't know, *massive*. I took it out for a spin. I do so hope it didn't inconvenience you."

As his eyes adjusted to the darkness, he got a good look at her for the first time. She was dressed all in black leather. Not exactly the fashion statement he would've expected from her.

She noticed his scrutiny. "Ah yes, the outfit. For a . . . er, costume party. Just trying it out. One never knows how leather will wear."

Barbara reached out for his hand. He gave it to her—albeit warily—and allowed her to help him to his feet.

"Nice throw," he said.

"Ah, yes," she replied. "Judo lessons at school. All the rage, you know. I suppose they've taken better than I thought." She smiled. "Again, my greatest of pardons."

Dick didn't have a chance to respond. Before he could even think about it, Barbara was gone, her withdrawal fueled by her profound embarrassment. Or was it something more than that? he wondered.

He stared at the bike she'd borrowed, then at her retreating figure, then at the bike again. All was not as it seemed in Wayne Manor.

CHAPTER

10

If Freeze had any real feelings left, if his heart hadn't frozen in his chest like a cold, dead relic of some ancient civilization, his humiliation might have been overwhelming.

Not just because he was headed for a cell in the notoriously hellish institution known as Arkham Asylum. Not because he was being put away with some of the most sadistic criminal minds ever to caress a switchblade.

No, it was the way in which he was being transported there.

Freeze had been jammed inside a giant, subzero refrigerator on a heavy-duty gurney, the door to the refrigerator chained and padlocked shut. Only his frost-covered face was visible through the opening formerly occupied by the freezer compartment door.

It allowed him to see where he was going as a couple of armed guards trundled him through the maximum-security wing. But it also allowed the other inmates to see *him,* and that was the part he would have found so humiliating if he were still a mere warm-blooded human being.

The place was dark and full of shrieking pleas for help. And it smelled of things Freeze was disinclined to think about.

Through the small, barred window set into the door of one cell, he could see a dark-bearded visage emerge from the shadows. And a moment later, an arrogant smile.

"It's good to see you, Lord of the Frigid North," the inmate declared in a resonant and commanding voice. "Perhaps we can join forces for a little revenge. As you know, it's a dish best served *cold.*"

Then he laughed. It was a sound to chill the blood—assuming one's vessels weren't already filled with cryogenic solution.

Freeze turned away and eyed a cell on the other side of the corridor. The inmate there was pressing his face against the bars as if trying to push his way out.

"I've got one for you," he whispered. "Listen up, okay? What d'ya get when you cross a magician with an icicle? Huh? Whaddaya get? No, really, what? Just *guess,* for godsakes."

As Freeze's conveyance passed the cell, the man grew more insistent. More desperate for an answer. But Freeze had no intention of taking part in his little game.

"All right," the man shrieked. "I'll tell, I'll tell. You get a cold spell, y'see? A *cold* spell!"

Freeze saw. He wasn't amused.

There were others. Not all of them talked. But all of them took notice of his passage.

"How d'ya like it?" sneered one of his guards. "You're the common cold, and we're the cure. Welcome home, Frost Face."

The prisoner rolled his eyes to look up at the man. "Allow me to break the ice," he said. "My name is *Freeze.* Learn it well, for it is the chilling sound of your own doom."

The guard chuckled. "Sure it is. That's what they all say." He indicated a cell with a tilt of his head. "The Hatter there? Said he'd fit me for a headband a few sizes too small. The Scarecrow? Promised he'd send me screaming into the night. But here I am. And there *they* are."

They stopped outside a cell door with no one looking out of its barred window. One of the guards turned a high-tech key in the stainless-steel lock, and the door swung open. Then they wheeled Mr. Freeze inside and dumped him out of his freezer onto the floor.

He had no suit on. But there was a mechanism in the middle of his cell that promised to remedy that oversight. Glowing rings on the floor and ceiling projected a shimmering column of snowy cold. A cold field, as it were. The guards began dragging him into it.

Suddenly, in a burst of icy fury, Freeze shrugged off the guards. Smashing one in the face with his fist, he kicked the other in the chest—and ran for the door.

An error in judgment, as it turned out. As his body left the hypothermic field, he felt a terrible searing pain in his insides. Tumbling to his knees, he looked at his hands. They were withering, turning gray, giving off a putrid mist. So was the rest of his body.

"Look at him stew," said one of the guards—the one with the big mouth. "How do you like your bad guy, Joey? Medium or well-done?"

The guards stood over Freeze and laughed as the villain tried to crawl back inside the field. No Olympic event had ever been so difficult for him, so charged with agony.

Finally, he made it inside. The pain began to subside. His color began to return to normal as well.

"Get used to it," snarled the guard. "You're gonna be here a long time, Freeze. A *very* long time."

The villain looked up at the guard, who had gone to the wall sink to wash his hands. Freeze smiled an empty smile.

"I'm afraid not," he said. "You see, the means of my liberation are in your hands. Sadly, you will not live to see it."

Ivy considered the Turkish bathhouse. It was a good site, centrally located in Gotham's theater district. And it was no longer in use, if the boards nailed across the front door were any indication.

Perfect, she thought. But truthfully, her mind wasn't entirely on the site-selection process.

"So those janitors at the Flower Ball were Batface and Birdbrain, militant arm of the warm-blooded oppressors." She grunted. "They turned out to be more resistant to my love dust than I would have expected."

She looked at Bane, who stood beside her with a satchel in hand, awaiting orders. He had nothing to say. No reaction to her comment.

"No matter," Ivy went on. "I'll give them a stronger dose next time. They'll literally be . . . *dying* for me."

Pointing to the door of the bathhouse, she told Bane: "Go to work."

Without hesitation, he dropped the satchel. Then he joined his fists and hammered his way through the wooden boards. Sturdy two-by-fours splintered like balsa wood.

Ivy led the way inside, Bane following with his satchel. Clearing away a cobweb, she could see that her assumption had been correct. The place was deserted. Abandoned by its previous occupants some time ago.

There was a large collection of Middle Eastern furniture, all of it stained and crumbling. Pictures of slaves and sycophants covered the cracked walls, their colors smudged and faded.

Ivy sighed. "A fixer-upper, yes. But with a certain homey charm."

That's when the shadows in the back of the place began to move. One slipped across the doorway. Several more surrounded them.

"Ah," said Ivy, "a minus. Current tenants."

One such tenant stepped into a column of moonlight projected through a hole in the roof. He was pale, but strong-looking in a stringy kind of way. His age? Somewhere between fifteen and twenty-five.

An urban predator, Ivy observed with the practiced eye of a scientist. His jacket labeled him one of the "Golums." In fact, these specimens seemed to have that in common.

"You boys ought to get out more," she advised them. "A little sun does wonders for the complexion."

"Hello, pretty," said the one who'd stepped forward.

"Hello yourself," Ivy replied. "I love this place, I really do. I hope it's priced to sell."

"We love *you*," Golum told her. "You look good enough to eat."

She laughed. "Oh, that I am. Come and get me—if you can."

The Golums closed in. Just as quickly, Ivy slammed the activation stud on Bane's chest. The pump in his backpack went to work, forcing Venom through the tubes on his back into his skull. He dropped his satchel again.

The Golums attacked. But Bane hurled them away effortlessly, the way a larger animal might toss a smaller one. He kicked them, punched them, and sent them hurtling into walls.

One by one, they slumped to the floor and lay still. And with each demise, the Golums' chances of beating Bane diminished.

Eventually, the survivors ran away. From Ivy's point of view, it was the smartest thing they had ever done.

She gazed at her servant approvingly. "For the strong, silent type, you can be most persuasive. Let's redecorate." She crossed the room, appraising it as she went. "First, the light is all wrong."

At another gesture from her, Bane ripped a hanging board from the ceiling. Old wooden planks tumbled to the floor, expanding the shaft of moonlight that streamed in from above.

"Also," said Ivy, "what is this floor?"

Bane stomped on it, revealing the dirt beneath.

"Au naturel," she said approvingly. "Still, I've always hankered for something on the water."

Bane found a water main and smashed it with his foot. Water gushed out, irrigating the soil and then some.

"Now a little color," Ivy decided. "As I understand it, it took God seven days to create paradise." She withdrew a handful of tiny seeds from Bane's satchel. "Let's see if I can do better."

Ivy dropped the tiny seeds on the ground. Instantly, they began to sprout into vines, which in turn spawned fast-budding flowers. She saw the *Welcome to Gotham* bauble in the satchel as well and removed it. Then she turned to face her accomplice.

"Bane," she said, "I've found a fellow who strikes my fancy. A cool customer, yes. Icy demeanor, no question. But I detect a certain ruthless charm I may be able to use to my advantage."

Glancing at the dead thugs all around her, she added, "Honey, clean up this mess, won't you? We've got company coming."

Alfred had set the table for dinner with his usual attention to detail. But in fact, his attention was a world away.

He had tried everything he could think of in his search for his brother Wilfred. It had availed him nothing. And time, unfortunately, was very much of the essence.

"Alfred?" said a decidedly feminine voice.

He emerged from his reverie with a start. "Yes, Miss Madison?" he responded, turning in the starlet's direction.

She smiled apologetically. "I was hoping for some more

wine," she said, indicating her nearly empty glass with an inclination of her head.

"Of course," he told her. Lifting the wine bottle from its place in the ice-filled wine bucket beside the table, he poured Julie Madison a refill. Then he turned to his employer.

"Sir?"

Bruce held up his hand. "None for me, Alfred. Thanks."

Restoring the bottle to its bucket, the butler walked away and allowed the two young people their privacy. However, he had barely exited the room when he felt another agonizing, gut-wrenching pang.

Reaching out for the wall, Alfred did his best to endure it. To get through it somehow. Sweat beaded on his forehead in testimony to his effort. A moan escaped his lips.

Finally, the pain went away. But it left him weak and trembling, even worse than before.

He had to find Wilfred, he told himself. Before it was too *late.*

Bruce watched Alfred head for the kitchen, then turned back to his guest. Ivy was sitting at the other end of the long table in the dining room of Wayne Manor, licking her lips with sensuous abandon.

"Bruce?" she asked.

But it wasn't Ivy who'd said his name. He blinked—and saw Julie sitting there, the glow of the fireplace discovering golden highlights in her hair.

Not Ivy. *Julie.*

She leaned forward. "You're not even listening to me, are you?"

"What?" said Bruce. "I'm sorry. You were saying . . ."

Julie frowned. "We've been going out over a year now

and . . . okay, here goes. Bruce, I want to spend my life with you."

Out of the corner of his eye, Bruce saw someone moving languidly in the background. Someone dressed all in green. Coming up behind him, she ran her hands down his chest.

Swallowing hard, Bruce got up and went over to Julie. But he wasn't so much approaching his guest as retreating from the vision of Ivy.

"Julie," he said, chuckling softly, even a little nervously, "I'm not the marrying kind. There are things about me you wouldn't understand."

She shrugged. "Like what? I know you're a dedicated bachelor. That you've had your wild nights."

"Wild doesn't exactly cover it," he said.

Julie took his hand. "But there's nothing you've done under the cover of darkness I couldn't learn to understand."

Bruce smiled uncomfortably. "I wouldn't bet on that."

"I'm betting on *you*," she told him, leaning closer.

He couldn't help but notice how her eyes sparkled in the candlelight. Or the muskiness of her perfume.

"You'll make someone a good husband one day," Julie predicted. "But I can't wait around forever. Don't answer now. Just promise me you'll think it over, all right?"

Then she leaned even closer, until her lips were only inches from his. "And here's some food for thought," she whispered.

Their lips met and they kissed. Passionately. After what seemed like a long time, Bruce opened his eyes.

And recoiled at the sight of Ivy.

But it was only Julie, he realized a second later. Only Julie, looking up at him with a puzzled expression.

"Who's Ivy?" she asked.

"What?" he blurted.

"You just called me Ivy. Who's Ivy?"

Bruce took a breath, let it out. "I wish I knew."

Dick Grayson sat and listened to loud, driving music and stared intently at the Batcave's computer monitors. The ones on the sides were blank. The one in the middle showed a newsphoto of the Flower Ball survivors.

"Enhance detail," he said. "Quadrants fourteen to nineteen."

A corner of the screen was highlighted. A moment later, the highlighted image was expanded to fill a larger portion of the screen.

It was a picture of Ivy.

Dick shook his head. "Who are you?" he asked out loud.

He was interrupted by the clanging of an alarm. Suddenly, the screen changed to an image of Barbara Wilson climbing out her window. As Dick got to his feet, he saw her start to rappel down an exterior wall of the manor. She was in her leathers again.

"Alert," said the computer. "Unauthorized motion within specified parameters. Repeat, alert."

Dick grinned. "Gotcha!"

He made it to the stairs in a couple of bounds. Then up the steps, through the house, out the door, and across the grounds that separated the mansion from the garage. What's more, he arrived in time to see her duck inside.

This time, he remained in the shadows as he watched Barbara wheel out the competition bike and straddle it. Kick-starting the engine, she peeled out into the night.

But not alone. Not this time. Rolling another racing bike out of the shadows, Dick pulled on his helmet, kicked his engine into life, and started after her.

Of course, he didn't catch up to her. Not right away, at

least. He hung back as far as he could without losing her, letting her lead him through the suburbs and into the city. By the time she was done, she was in one of the worst parts of Gotham.

A broad, cobblestoned street in what used to be the meat-packing district. But the packing plants had closed a long time ago, and no one lived here now except the rodents.

Several motorcycle riders had gathered there, each representing a different gang. Some had dyed their hair, others had pierced their faces. All were leather-clad, though their costumes varied. Boys and girls for whom speed was a drug, the streets their second home.

Dick recognized the bikers' colors. Some, he'd seen close up. Others, he knew from the files Batman kept on them. If Bruce hadn't taken him in after the death of his family, Dick might easily have become one of them.

"... *my rules.*"

Frowning, he put the thought aside and focused on the job at hand. Just as he had on the statue, he assured himself.

With a quick burst of speed, Barbara pulled up alongside one of the bikers—someone named Banker, if memory served. Top dog in a west-side gang called the Disciples.

Banker looked Barbara up and down. "Whassup?"

"How much coin to play?" she asked.

"Two and a half," he grunted.

She nodded and produced the cash. Banker tucked it into a hidden pocket in his racing leathers.

Another biker stepped forward. His street name was Spike.

"You got a tag?" he asked Barbara.

She shrugged. "Folks call me Three-Jump."

Spike's eyes narrowed. "You're the slice won the tunnel run two nights ago. That was trike racing. This is the stuff." He grinned. "Maybe you wanna ride my hog instead."

Barbara returned the smile. "How about a side bet?"

The other bikers oohed and aahed. They were impressed.

Spike stopped grinning. "You're on," he spat. "How's another five hundred sound, slice?"

"Sounds good," she said.

Banker held the cash for both of them. As he tucked it away in his outfit, Dick moved his bike forward and paid his entry fee. His face hidden by his helmet, there was no way Barbara would be able to tell who he was.

The racers all donned their headgear and assumed their starting positions. Engines revved. Banker raised a pistol in the air . . .

. . . and fired.

Suddenly, the bikers shot down the street. Some went over the tops of cars, others across cement stoops. Dick saw a biker beside Barbara career into a pile of trash cans, sending them flying every which way.

Two others went neck and neck toward an oncoming truck. At the last possible second, they split up and flew off parked cars, then converged and hit the ground again. But one of them spun out, allowing the other to take a position at the head of the pack.

Nice race, thought Dick.

But that didn't stop him from creeping ahead to join the leaders. After all, that's where Alfred's niece was, and he wanted to be able to keep an eye on her.

After a couple of minutes, he pulled even with Barbara, Spike, and another racer, leaving the rest of the bikers in his dust. Then one of the front-runners hit a patch of oil and skidded into a wall, turning himself and his bike into a raging fireball.

Dick winced. That could've been any of them.

Up ahead, he could see the finish line—a series of

flashing yellow warning beacons. They were situated atop
the incomplete construction of a drawbridge in the near
distance.

The race was really down to three now—Barbara,
Spike, and him. They raced onto the bridge, jockeying for
position with riveted steel clanking beneath their wheels.

The finish line was coming up fast. But just beyond the
line of flashing cones, there was an abyss separating the
two as-yet-unconnected components of the bridge. The
trick was to cross the finish line first, but still avoid pitch-
ing into the water just past it.

Spike was keeping up fine, but he was approaching the
finish line too fast. Choosing the better part of valor, he hit
his brakes—slowing himself down and effectively falling
out of contention.

Dick could see Barbara turn to look at him. Showing no
sign of recognition, she turned back to the finish line and
gunned her engine. He did the same.

Barbara flew over the line, Dick a hair behind her. Then
both of them shot over the edge of the unfinished bridge
into the air, soaring high above the watery gap.

Dick's front wheel hit the metal roadway on the other
side of the gap. Spinning rubber caught cold, hard steel.
Home free, he looked back to see about Barbara.

Unfortunately, her back wheel hadn't cleared the road
surface. It had hit the roadway's front edge. Barbara's bike
was losing purchase, slipping backward over the brink.

In one motion, Dick ditched his still-moving bike and
his helmet. Then he leaped toward the edge of the roadway
as Barbara's bike finally slipped. She and her hog both
tumbled into the abyss.

Straining, Dick stretched out as far as he could. His
hand reached out and caught Barbara's ankle. Then his
feet sought the lip of the bridge.

For a moment, it wasn't clear—even to Dick—if he'd
caught the lip. As if to underline the question, Barbara's

helmet fell off and plunged into the dark waters after her bike.

But *they* didn't. They dangled there, Dick hanging from one foot as he supported both their weights.

"So *this* is where you hang out," he quipped.

CHAPTER

11

The night before, at the tunnel run, Barbara had been exhilarated, flushed with victory. Though she'd won this race as well, her feelings at the moment were completely different.

". . . eighteen-fifty, nineteen hundred, nineteen-fifty, two thousand," said Banker. As Spike looked on, he handed her the last of the crumpled fifty-dollar bills. "Don't spend it all in one place, girlfriend."

Unfortunately, she thought, she would have to do just that. Turning, she saw that Dick had righted his bike and was waiting for her across the street. With a sigh of resignation, she approached him.

"I could have made it," Barbara told him, though she wasn't sure she believed it herself. "I didn't need your help, you know."

He shrugged carelessly. "Whatever you say, lady. It's all in a day's work for me."

She offered Dick her winnings. "Here. This is a down payment on the bike I lost. I'll get you the rest."

Dick looked at the money, then shook his head. "Nah. Keep it."

Barbara frowned. "Of course. Dick Grayson, ward of

the fabulously wealthy Bruce Wayne. Why would you need a few hundred dollars? You probably tip that much at lunch."

"Hey," said Dick, holding his hands out in an appeal for reason, "what's your problem? I didn't bite you, I saved your life."

She had to admit he had a point. "All right. My apologies. I guess the truth is I'm not comfortable with the idle rich. Even when they try to act like heroes."

He absorbed that, then patted the back of his seat. "Well, you better get comfortable real fast, sister. 'Cause we've only got one bike between us now, and it's a long walk home."

Needless to say, she chose the ride. It wasn't so bad, either. Dick knew Gotham a lot better than she did, and he took them down a couple of scenic routes she would otherwise have missed.

By the time they got back to Wayne Manor, she felt more gratitude than resentment. And more relief than embarrassment.

When they reached the garage, they dismounted. "So what's this Three-Jump stuff?" Dick asked.

"A race I got into in London," she explained. "It's a long story."

He eyed her. "So who am I talking to? Ms. Oxbridge or Three-Jump? Who are you really?"

"Both," she said. "Neither. I don't really know."

A funny expression came over Dick's face. "You'd be amazed at just how common that is around here."

"I started racing after my parents died," Barbara explained, entirely without provocation. She believed she owed him that. "There was something about the speed, the danger, that took me out of myself—that made the hurt go away for a while."

He looked at her, declining to comment.

"You wouldn't understand," she said.

Dick quirked a sad, little smile. "You'd be surprised."

Encouraged, she went on. "Street racing isn't an acceptable major at Oxbridge. They kicked me out. It doesn't matter, though. I've won enough money to do what I've always dreamed."

He regarded her narrow-eyed. "Just don't tell me you're hoping to run away and join the circus."

Barbara left the garage and headed for the entrance to the house. Dick walked along with her.

"Uncle Alfred has supported me my whole life," she said. "Given me everything I needed. Now I'm going to pay him back. I'm going to liberate him from his dismal life of servitude."

Dick laughed. "What are you talking about?" Suddenly, he seemed like the rich boy again.

She felt herself growing indignant. "Servants, masters . . . it's ridiculous," she told him. "Alfred is the sweetest, most noble man alive, and he's subjugated all his life and dreams to someone else."

As they walked into the darkened house, her companion shook his head. "Alfred and Bruce aren't like that. They're more like family."

Barbara made a sound of disdain. "Paying someone to prepare your meals and do your laundry and clean your dishes, to wait on you hand and foot—you call that family?"

Dick shrugged. "Alfred's happy here."

"Happy." She shook her head bitterly. "You honestly don't know, do you? You can't even see what's in front of your eyes?"

They had reached the stairway. Dick stared at her, clearly at a loss.

"Look at his skin," said Barbara. "At how he's hiding the pain all the time. Can't you see it? Alfred's *sick*."

Dick's brow creased, but he didn't say anything. He just

stood there, absorbing what was obviously a revelation to him.

Leaving him that way, she ran up the stairs.

Dick stared after Barbara as she took the stairs two at a time. *Alfred*, he thought . . . *sick*? It didn't seem to want to sink in.

"Alfred's not sick."

He whirled and saw it was Bruce who had spoken. The older man was standing in the shadows beside the stairs. Emerging from the darkness, he sat down on the lowest step.

"He's not?" Dick said hopefully.

Bruce shook his head. "No. He's dying." A pause. "And I can't seem to deal with it."

The boy felt a wave of emotion coming on. He swallowed it back. "But he never said a word—"

"You know Alfred. He'd never say anything. But I can tell." Bruce's eyes glinted in the darkness, reflecting some faraway light. "Until you came along, Alfred was the only family I ever had. I don't know how I would have survived without him. He saved my life, Dick. And I never told him."

Dick could feel the weight on Bruce's shoulders as if it were on his own. "Talk to him," he advised. "Tell Alfred how you feel. There's nothing worse than losing someone without . . ."

He had to stop. There was a lump in his throat.

". . . without telling them how you feel," he got out.

For what seemed like a long time, Bruce sat there at the bottom of the steps, looking more like a little boy than the larger-than-life Batman, protector of Gotham.

"I know," he said at last.

Mr. Freeze knelt in his cell, careful to remain within the parameters of the antithermic field that had been specially designed for him, and crafted a tiny ice sculpture of his wife. Lifting the miniature gearworks from an alarm clock on the floor beside him, he placed the ice statuette on top of it.

Then he flicked a switch and watched the sculpture begin to turn.

That's when he heard the sound of footsteps down the hall. Quickly, he covered the ice figure with a drinking glass.

"Hey, Icehead!" shouted a guard as he poked his head into view. "Want a drink?" He produced a water pitcher and a cup. "Incoming."

Laughing, the guard tossed a cupful of water at Freeze. Predictably, the liquid turned to a hunk of snow as it crossed the energy field—and hit the prisoner in the face.

Dispassionately, Freeze gathered the frost and used it to add a detail to the sculpture. He glanced at the guard.

"Your death will be a slow one," he said flatly.

"Yeah. And the Knights'll win the World Series. Dream on, Snowflake."

A tone sounded. The guard picked up his intercom earphone and plugged it in. Listening for a beat, he walked over to a control panel set into the wall and hit a button.

"You got a visitor," he told the prisoner. "Looks like your sister's here to see you."

"Sister?" echoed Freeze. He *had* no sister.

Then another guard showed up, followed by a woman in a green cloak. Freeze had seen her before, at the Flower Ball. What was her name again?

Ah yes. Poison Ivy.

Chuckie Kochman had been a guard at Arkham for nearly three years. He thought it was the greatest job in the world.

Of course, not all the other guards shared his enthusiasm. They had to watch the prisoners, make sure they were fed and clothed, and go after them when they tried to get away.

Which, for some reason, happened an awful lot.

But Chuckie's job was different. It was up to him to keep track of the lockup where the prisoners' personal effects were kept.

In the lockup, it seemed like every day was Halloween. Hanging on this rack were the Mad Hatter's threads. Hanging there was the Riddler's outfit, somewhere else the Scarecrow's.

And in another place, the latest entry—the big, silver playsuit worn by the esteemed Mr. Freeze.

Like they really needed someone to guard the stuff. Like the suits were going to dust themselves off and go release the guys who used to wear them. Like Chuckie might, even once, have to turn off the TV to do something more strenuous than reach for some cheese puffs.

Speaking of which . . .

The glare of the television on his face, Chuckie reached back and grabbed another handful of puffs. He loved this show, the one where the dad was Frankenstein and the grandfather was a fat old vampire and the little boy was a werewolf in short pants.

And the dad, the Frankenstein guy, was so big and so clumsy he could break a wall just by stumbling into it.

Of course, even that guy would have had a hard time breaking into Chuckie's lockup. The walls here in Arkham's basement were made of concrete a foot thick. And the only window to the hallway was a little barred one, barely big enough to see through.

Chuckie tossed back the cheese puffs, then brushed off his hands. Greatest job in the world, all right.

Suddenly, something crashed through the concrete wall beside him and grabbed him by the throat. He groped for his gun, but something grabbed him by the wrist then as well.

A pair of hands. Huge, powerful hands.

As his air was cut off and his face started to swell with constricted blood, Chuckie caught a glimpse of a black leather mask and a pair of bloodshot eyes—the scariest eyes he had ever seen.

Then the hand around his throat strangled the life out of him.

Ivy attracted her share of scrutiny from the inmates as she negotiated Arkham's infamous maximum-security corridor. There were catcalls and whistles, which was more or less what she expected.

What she didn't expect—what she found slightly unnerving, she had to admit—were the silent cells. The ones from which all she got were furtive stares. And in one case, a smacking of the lips.

Still, she took it as a compliment. Even more so when she considered how little of her they actually saw, with her hat, her cloak, and her dark glasses concealing her charms as much as anything could.

The two guards escorting her the length of the cell block weren't affected the way the inmates were. But then, they'd probably seen a woman sometime in the last several months. Many of the men behind these triple-thick steel doors would have drooled over Gossip Gerty.

"I love you," chortled a drooling specimen in a strait-jacket. "Let's do dinner. And then breakfast."

At one of the barred openings in the cell doors, all she saw was the glint of a mirror in an empty top hat. And a big, curious eyeball reflected in it, staring hungrily at her.

"Won't you join the dance?" asked a voice from inside the same cell. A harsh, gravelly voice. "Or at least tell me, like a good little girl . . . why is a raven like a writing desk?"

"Hey, Buster," bellowed another inmate, red-faced with indignation. "*I* ask the riddles around here!"

"Riddle me *this*, ya freakin' nutjob!"

"Shut up, the whole two of ya!"

"Pay no attention to them," said yet another of the inmates—a man with a dark, curly beard. His voice was that of a man used to being obeyed. "Open this door, my sweet. Free me from Hades and I'll place you beside me on Olympus. We'll make my wife Hera jealous as all get-out."

Ivy smiled inwardly at their antics. *Good*, she thought. *Let them eat their hearts out.*

Before long, she and her escort came to Mr. Freeze's cell. By then, she thought, her henchman should have been well about his business.

The guards opened the door and let her in, then joined her. Freeze was standing in a circle of shimmering light in the center of the cell, eyeing all three of them warily.

The guards sealed the door with a special key and remained there. "Don't mind us, ma'am," one of them snickered. "Go ahead and converse as freely as you like."

Apparently, there was no privacy to be had in a place like this. *Oh well*, she thought. She would create her own.

Ivy sized up the guards, then approached them. "I don't mind you at all," she told them.

She removed her hat and sunglasses, revealing her intensely green eyes. The guards' eyes opened wide in return.

"You're not all that attractive," she went on, pulling her hair out of its bun so it could fall around her shoulders. "Pretty average, I'd say. But your fantasies aren't average, are they?"

Ivy began to saunter around the room. Little by little, teasing them, she shed her cloak to reveal her skintight green costume.

"Your fantasies are anything *but* average," she continued. "The things you think about late at night when you're all alone. I understand them. I want them. I *am* them."

Her circuit around the room brought her back to the guards. They were thoroughly mesmerized.

"Men," she sighed. "The most absurd of all God's creatures. We women give you life, and we can take it back just as easily."

Ivy took one guard's chin in each of her hands. Then she leaned in close enough to plant a kiss.

"What if I told you one kiss from me would kill you?" she asked.

"Right," said one guard.

"Whatever," said the other.

"I really *am* to die for," she remarked.

Then she kissed them, both of them, each in turn. There was a moment of pure, undiluted bliss on their faces. Then they choked, fell to their knees, and died horribly.

Freeze nodded from his circle of light. "Impressive."

Ivy looked at him and smiled seductively. "Well, I, my most Unabominable Snowman, have been impressed by *you*. In fact, I propose a pairing. And in the interest of that pairing, I'm here to set you free."

Freeze considered her. "An enticing offer," he decided. "But what does the lady want in return?"

What indeed? she thought. But this was neither the time nor the place.

"Let's cool it for now," she told him reluctantly. "There's someone I would like you to meet."

Ivy knelt and unhooked the key from the guard's belt. Then she used it to unlock the door. It opened. Right on cue, Bane walked in, carrying Freeze's silver thermosuit. Then Ivy sealed the door behind him.

"His name is Bane," she said.

"Ah," said Freeze. "A laundry service that delivers. Thank you, Mr. Bane."

Bane didn't answer. He just tossed the suit to Freeze through the boundaries of the cryonic field. Snatching it out of the air, Freeze began to pull it on eagerly.

"I love that belt," Ivy told him frankly. "What are you, about a fifty big and tall?"

Freeze chuckled dryly. "I always go a size smaller," he said. "Makes me look slimmer."

He glanced at the various components of his suit, checking them off one by one. Everything seemed to be in order until he inspected his watchlike status display. Then his expression changed.

Ivy looked at the device herself and saw that Freeze was on auxiliary power. Dangerously low, no doubt.

Freeze opened his sleeve compartments. They were empty.

He muttered a curse. "They've confiscated my generator diamonds. I'm running on empty."

Outside, they could hear the shouts of approaching guards. Soon, the flame of a laser torch could be seen cutting around the perimeter of the cell's steel door.

Ivy hit the pump on Bane's back. Milky white Venom flowed through his tubes and surged into his system.

Bane lifted his fists and tried to smash the wall farthest from the entrance. It didn't break.

She shook her head. "Not good. Not good at all."

They heard the shouts of more guards coming down

the hall. Freeze reached for his holster—obviously out of instinct, because it was empty.

"No gun," he muttered. "How disarming."

Ivy frowned. What was the worst that could happen? she asked herself. "I wonder if I can get a cell with a view of the gardens?"

Freeze shook his head. "Don't despair, dear Daisy." Having said that, he left the shelter of his antithermic field and crossed to a sink protruding from the cell wall.

He turned on the cold water. Then, cracking his gauntlet seal, he caused cryo-gas to come hissing out.

Freeze glanced back over his shoulder at Ivy. "What a boon is cold, for it allows a thing's true potential to be revealed. Take simple water—soft, pliant, ever so yielding. But freeze it and it grows resistant. Powerful. Harder than steel itself."

He aimed his gas jet at the spigot. One by one, the pipes around the room began to freeze, to frost over, to bulge— the frozen water within them finally splitting the metal. And the whole effect rushed headlong toward the stone wall opposite the door.

All at once, the wall began to crack. To crumble. More and more, until great chunks fell out of it, revealing the starry night sky outside Freeze's little cell.

Ivy took a step toward the opening and saw that they were in a turreted tower, far above the black and mysterious Gotham River.

"I hate heights," she groaned.

On the other side of the cell, the door flew off its hinges. The guards wouldn't be far behind.

"You'll hate prison more," Freeze advised her.

She supposed he was right. Holding her nose, she jumped.

As far as she could tell, Freeze and Bane were right behind her, plummeting toward the fast-rushing waters below.

CHAPTER

12

Bruce was walking with Alfred through the expansive first floor of Wayne Manor, shutting off the lights that hadn't already been shut off. He glanced at the man who had been mother and father to him, and it hurt him to think that man was in pain.

Alfred must have noticed his scrutiny, because his eyes slid toward Bruce. Along with his brows, they formed a question. "Sir?"

The younger man answered it with a question of his own. "Are you all right, Alfred?"

The butler thrust out his chin. He had to see that his jig was up—that there was no further possibility of hiding it. "As well as can be expected," he replied stoically.

Bruce sighed. "Alfred, I know you're sick. I can get you the best doctors. Anyone you need."

His friend—his oldest friend—shook his head. "I've already seen the best doctors, sir." And then: "A gentleman does not discuss his health. It's not civilized. I hope I've taught you that much, Master Bruce."

Bruce bit back a bitter smile. He knew better than to push Alfred when he was in this frame of mind.

Silence, as they turned off the lights in the living room. Then in the home office. And the parlor.

Finally, they got to the stairs. Bruce's room was on the second floor, Alfred's on the first. It was where they parted company.

"Will there be anything else?" the butler asked dutifully.

"A question," Bruce replied. "Alfred, have you ever regretted your life working here?"

The older man looked at him—and smiled. "Attending to heroes? No, sir. My only regret is that I was never able to be out there with you."

"Not all heroes wear masks," Bruce reminded him.

"I suppose that's true," Alfred agreed.

The billionaire put his hand on his friend's shoulder. "Alfred," he said, "if I've never told you . . . I just want to say . . ."

"Yes?" the butler prompted.

Bruce swallowed, fighting tears. For all his willpower, for all his inner strength, he was unable to speak the words.

He found himself looking past Alfred for a moment. Looking out the window, into the distance.

What he saw was not the dark of night, but the light of day. And a game. A boy—young Bruce, himself—was playing hide-and-seek with his middle-aged manservant. Alfred disappeared behind a hedge and then appeared again. And the boy laughed.

Remembering where he was, Bruce turned back to Alfred. "I want to say . . ." he began again.

But before he could finish, he heard footfalls—someone running. A moment later, Dick sprang into sight. He spoke three words.

"Freeze has escaped."

Bruce went to the window and craned his neck to gaze in the direction of the city center. He could see the Bat-Signal shining against the clouds in the night sky.

His signal.

"Come on," he told Dick. He would speak to Alfred later, he promised himself. "Let's go."

Freeze sat in a limousine filled with flowers, Ivy ensconced beside him and Bane at the wheel. As they drove by the Snowy Cones Ice Cream Factory, he peered out between roses and chrysanthemums. The place was surrounded now by a police perimeter.

"My reserves are exhausted," he complained. "I must have the gems that power my suit."

And that wasn't his only problem. Nora was inside the factory, too.

Ivy glanced at him. "You *are* looking unseasonably hot. Let's go inside and grab your rocks."

Suddenly, they saw the Batmobile arrive, tires screeching. Batman and Robin raced inside the factory.

Damn, thought Freeze. "In my weakened state," he said miserably, "I am no match for the Bat and the Bird."

"You leave Batman and Robin to me," said Ivy.

Freeze looked at her, unable to conceal his skepticism. She smiled.

"Trust me. Vegetable magnetism."

Freeze nodded. After all, she seemed so confident.

"Fine," he said. "While I retrieve my diamonds, you and Meatloaf will bring my wife to your lair. She's frozen in—"

Ivy's demeanor changed suddenly. She seemed to be . . . a tad jealous.

"Hold it," she told him. "Stop the music. You never said anything about a wife, frozen or otherwise."

It only confirmed what Freeze had suspected—that the green woman wished to engage him in a love affair. But to Freeze, such a thing was unthinkable. He loved his wife no less now than the day they were married. And if it meant walking over the bodies of a thousand Ivys to bring Nora back, he would do that without hesitating.

Moving quickly, he grabbed Ivy by her throat and smashed her back into her padded seat. Bane turned to stop him, but the green woman shooed him away with an extraordinarily casual gesture.

"You will rescue my wife," Freeze grated. "Without her, the world has no beauty. No reason for me to go on. When I have found the cure for the disease that robbed her from me, when she is warm in my arms again, I will repay you for your efforts as you see fit."

"Okay, okay," Ivy rasped, her windpipe partially obstructed by his grip. "Poison Ivy to the rescue. Now, where do I find your brittle bride?"

He told her everything she needed to know.

Batman looked around what had been Freeze's lair. The police had everything tagged and taped, as they should have. But of course, there was still a lot more to be unearthed from this frigid ground.

Commissioner Gordon, once called "the second-toughest man in Gotham" by a reporter, walked into the room. Acknowledging Batman with a nod, he handed him a bunch of glossy photographs.

"There's no sign Freeze came back here after the breakout," Gordon explained. He pointed to the topmost photo. "We pulled that one off the surveillance cameras at Arkham."

Batman glanced at it. It showed Freeze, Ivy, and Ivy's big, leather-masked henchman making a daring dive into the Gotham River.

Gordon handed him another picture. "From the security camera at the Gotham Airport. Two nights ago."

This image was grainier than the other one. A woman

in a veiled hat and black widow's cloak stood next to a giant blurred form, also disguised with street clothes.

"These two," said Gordon, "arrived on a charter from South America. They put ten security guards in the hospital, left a businessman dead of organic poisoning, broke the neck of a chauffeur and stole his limousine." He paused. "Apparently, the big one is called Bane. One of the inmates overheard the name."

Batman nodded appraisingly. "Definitely the same pair that sprang Freeze."

As Gordon left, Robin came over to peer at the pictures as well. The younger man whistled softly.

"It's Poison Ivy all right."

"But why," asked Batman, "would she help Freeze to escape?"

"She's definitely evil," Robin observed. His face took on sterner lines. "You know, it's weird, but for a while Ivy was all I could think about. It was almost as if I loved her. But then . . ."

Batman grunted. "I know. The feeling just vanished."

Robin looked at him apologetically. He lowered his voice, so only his mentor could hear. "I can't believe we were fighting over a bad guy."

Batman frowned. "Bad, yes. Guy, no. This is one extraordinarily beautiful evil person."

Robin shrugged. "Beautiful or not, I'm totally over her. Positively."

"Same here," said Batman. But he couldn't help staring at her image a moment longer before shutting down the console.

"I'll be outside if you need me," said Gordon.

The Dark Knight nodded. His next step was to visit the walk-in freezer. Naturally, Robin followed him in.

Batman walked along a wall of frozen dinners, running the fingertips of his glove along their forward edges. Finally, he stopped at one dinner in particular—an Oriental one—and withdrew it from its place.

Abruptly, the door to a hidden vault swung open. He saw Robin look at him in amazement.

"How did you . . . ?"

By way of an explanation, Batman showed him the frozen dinner in his hand. "Open Sesame . . . Chicken."

Robin smiled. "Gotcha."

Entering the vault, Batman looked around—and saw the bizarre, high-tech sarcophagus that dominated the place. As he approached it, he realized there was someone inside.

It was Nora Fries.

"She's still alive," Batman observed. "Her husband was able to adapt his freezing technology to arrest McGregor's Syndrome." Glancing at a nearby monitor, he grunted appreciatively. "Freeze has even found a cure for the early stages of the disease."

"Can he save her?" asked Robin.

Batman shook his head from side to side. "Her case is too advanced. But maybe someday, with more research—"

He stopped himself, noticing the fairylike spirals that were beginning to wind their way through the room. He tried not to breathe them in, but he was already feeling a bit dazed.

Beckoning to Robin, he traced the dust spirals to a narrow, snaking passage at the far end of the vault. Following it, Batman found a pair of service doors. He wrenched them open.

Beyond the doors, Bane was standing atop a metal staircase, overlooking an industrial basement where catwalks crisscrossed above huge mixing vats and conveyor belts. As the crime fighters watched, the giant hit a switch and brought the machinery whirring to life.

So far, he hadn't seemed to notice their arrival.

"No beauty . . ." Batman whispered.

"Just the beast," Robin added.

Batman rushed Bane, hoping to capitalize on the element of surprise. It didn't work.

The monster saw him coming and moved faster than anyone his size had a right to. Sideswiping Batman, he sent him flying off the stairs toward the basement floor below.

But the Dark Knight didn't land on any floor. He came down in a mammoth ice-cream mixer. And before he knew it, a giant stirring arm was making a deadly sweep in his direction.

As he flipped himself out of the vat to avoid it, he could see that Robin was following up on his attack, smashing into Bane's chest with both feet. But the boy bounced off and came down hard atop the landing.

"Ouch," said Robin. "Any more at home like you?"

Bane didn't answer. He just advanced on the boy, his huge arms held out like a wrestler's.

Batman would have vaulted back up to the landing to help. But suddenly he found someone blocking his way, someone green and lovely and impossibly desirable.

Ivy smiled and blew a handful of dust in his face. "I must confess," she said, "the combination of derring-do and an anatomically correct rubber suit puts fire in a girl's . . . lips."

Up on the landing, Robin and Bane were battling it out. It was a fight Robin couldn't hope to win, but he was giving it everything he had.

A part of Batman knew he had to lend a hand, or his protégé would be pummeled to death. It was only a small part of him, but it wouldn't be overcome. He wouldn't let it.

As Ivy leaned in to kiss him, he recoiled. She seemed surprised.

"Why," Batman asked, dazed by her, "do all the gorgeous ones have to be homicidal maniacs? Is it me?"

"I'd turn over a new leaf," she said. "For the right man."

Suddenly, she took a swing at his face. He caught her wrist.

"Oh." She chuckled. "You like it rough." She tried to pull him close again. "Good," she said. "So do I."

Up above, Bane had gotten his hands on Robin and was spinning the boy over his head. Releasing Ivy—albeit reluctantly—Batman raced up the steps, taking them three at a time.

But he was a split second too late. The giant hurled Robin just as Batman smashed into him. Together, he and Bane fell off the platform, taking their fight to a catwalk below.

Out of the corner of his eye, Batman could see that Robin was all right. He had landed on a platform just a few feet lower down.

Thank God for small favors, he thought, as he ducked a blow from Bane that would've caved in his skull.

Scrambling to his feet, Robin found himself in front of a huge miller's wheel, which was carrying planks of wood through a chopper for conversion into Popsicle sticks.

"Hey, pretty birdie," said a seductive, feminine voice.

Turning, he saw Ivy in front of him. Before he could do anything, she blew a pile of dust in his face. Then she began advancing on him, backing Robin toward the chopper blades.

"No," he said, trying like hell to fight his revived attraction for her. "You're evil."

"Evil?" she repeated. "No. Just misguided. Basically I'm your garden-variety pretty girl."

"Turn yourself in," he insisted, though his heart wasn't in it. "If you threw yourself—"

"At you?" she suggested. Her green eyes sparkled suggestively.

"On the mercy of the court. Maybe they'd . . . I don't know. Release you into my custody." Even as he said it, he realized how unlikely it was.

She stroked his cheek. "So young. So sweet. And a hero to boot. I've wanted you from the first moment I saw you." Ivy leaned forward, lips pursed. "Polly want a kiss?"

Robin wanted to kiss her. He really did. But before he could even think about giving in to her charms, he heard a vicious crack above him.

Turning, he saw Batman stagger backward on a catwalk, reeling from one of Bane's blows. As the boy watched, Bane lurched forward and drove his fist into Batman's jaw, staggering him a second time.

The Dark Knight was dangerously close to the edge of the catwalk. Forgetting Ivy, Robin grabbed a strut on the miller's wheel—and the giant cog lifted him up toward Batman.

Down below, he could hear Ivy's exclamation of frustration. "I must be losing my touch," she complained.

Freeze was standing at the top of a stairway, not yet having reached the vault where he kept his most precious possessions . . . when the front doors to the factory blew open, revealing Commissioner Gordon and a squad of cops.

The villain glowered at them. "I hate uninvited guests."

As the cops raced up the stairs to get him, he pulled a lever marked COOLANT GAS. Suddenly, vents all around the room began hissing a freezing, blue gas.

The cops tried to fight their way through it, but Freeze had another surprise for them. "Why don't you boys slip into something more comfortable?" he asked—and pulled another lever.

Instantly, the steps were transformed into a steep, curving ramp, slick with a veneer of coolant-created ice. To put the icing on the cake, Freeze reached out and punched Gordon in the mouth, sending him tumbling backward into his shivering cohorts. The bunch of them went down like tenpins and slipped to the floor below.

With the cops momentarily disposed of, the villain resumed his journey to the diamond vault. Suddenly, another contingent of cops emerged from one of the blue-gas clouds.

This time, Freeze didn't resort to any technotricks—just to his own strength and lightning reflexes. Whipping billy clubs from the holsters of two police, he used them like a set of Filipino escrima sticks, knocking the cops unconscious with a flurry of slams and jabs.

"Stick around," he told them grimly, as he sent the cops flying in opposite directions.

One of them disappeared into another cloud of gas. The other one hit a wall. Beside him, a button read EMERGENCY HEAT.

A bad move, thought Freeze.

Somehow, the cop found the presence of mind to reach up and slam the stud. All over the room, gray filaments came to life. The place began to glow a vibrant red.

Just then, Freeze's watch started flashing. He held it up to his eyes and felt his heart sink. *No power.*

As Ivy watched, Bane kicked Batman off the end of their catwalk. But before her gigantic servant could revel in his victory—even if he were capable of such a thing— Robin leaped onto his massive back.

Robin wasn't Batman, but he seemed to know what he

was doing. And he was nothing if not game. For a little while, at least, it seemed Bane would have his hands full with him.

In the meantime, Batman himself landed on his back on a slow-moving conveyor belt—one that was feeding ancient tubs of ice cream into a clown-shaped flash freezer. Ivy jumped on top of the crime fighter and lowered her face close to his.

"You bring out the animal in me," she told him.

"I should have brought my leash," he replied.

Ivy grunted. "Enough sweet talk."

With that, she blew another handful of dust into his face—and licked her lips. She would enjoy this, she thought. Oh, how she would enjoy this. Slowly, she leaned in for a kiss.

But at the last possible moment, just before her lips brushed against Batman's, he averted his face and wrenched her to the conveyor belt—just ahead of the clown's freezing maw.

"You're going to jail," he declared.

Ivy marveled at his resolve. After all, her powder was powerful stuff. It must have taken a superhuman effort to resist it.

"I'm a lover," she said, "not a fighter. That's why every Poison Ivy action figure comes complete with . . . *him*."

She pointed to Bane, who was standing atop a giant storage vat, a dazed Robin hanging like a rag doll in his hands. As Ivy and Batman watched, Bane tossed Robin aside and slid feetfirst down another conveyor belt—right *at* them.

Batman didn't move as quickly as Ivy had seen him move before. Before he could react, Bane crashed into him. Then, carried by the giant's momentum, the two of them smashed into the wall with bone-crushing force.

Ivy waved good-bye to Batman as she swung down off the belt. "I'm off to find Bachelor Number Two," she announced. "Try not to make too much of a mess when you die."

Freeze could feel the room he was in getting hotter by the second. He staggered in the direction of his vault, his vitality ebbing fast, his flesh already beginning to turn gray.

With his last ounce of strength, Freeze ripped open his safe and filled his sleeve compartments with diamonds. Immediately, he could feel himself revitalized, feel his color returning.

"Ahh," he said. "Chilled to perfection."

Then he hit his watch. Suddenly, he was encased in ice. *Perfection indeed*, he thought.

Down below, the cops appeared to have recovered. They drew their guns and fired at him. But their bullets bounced off his icy armor, ricocheting into the walls.

He grinned savagely. "Superman, eat your heart out."

Then he headed for his weapons locker.

Dazed by his sudden introduction to the wall, Batman got his feet under him and tried to shake off the effects of Bane's attack. But the giant was on him again before he knew it.

A second time, he smashed Batman into the wall. As the Dark Knight slumped to the floor, Bane advanced on him for the coup de grâce. But Batman wasn't about to call it quits.

Reaching into his Utility Belt, he whipped out a Batclub and sent it whirling in Bane's direction. The club hit the giant in the head, stunning him, forcing him to take a couple of steps back into a rail.

Batman had earned himself a respite, though he had a feeling it would be all too brief. And out of the corner of his eye, he saw Ivy closing in on his protégé.

As the police rushed him, Freeze opened his locker and took out a small icing jewel. Using it on the floor, he watched the surface glow a brilliant blue and then cover over with ice.

The cops couldn't control their headlong progress over that kind of surface. Slipping on the icy floor in classic Keystone style, arms pinwheeling, they ended up sprawled on their backs.

Freeze stood, pulsing with power again. Removing a spare cryo-rifle from a pedestal nearby, he tucked it into the crook of his shoulder and pointed it at the helpless police.

"All right, coppers." He smiled humorlessly. "*Freeze.*"

Then he fired, just in case.

Rising to his feet and keeping one eye on Bane, Batman watched Ivy back Robin up against a giant vat.

"Stop living in the shadow of the big, bad Bat," she told him. "You don't need him." She blew more of her dust in his face. "You deserve your own legend, don't you?"

"My own . . . ?" he muttered.

"Your own bright, shining signal in the cloud-streaked sky. Let me guide you, brave heart. Let me . . ." She touched his face with her fingertips. ". . . touch you. Kiss you . . ."

It didn't seem Robin could resist her anymore. He was at her mercy—until Batman hurled a tiny Batarang with pinpoint accuracy, hitting his protégé in the cheek.

Fortunately, Bane was still woozy. He was hanging back, gathering his prodigious strength.

"Remember the victim at the airport," the Dark Knight shouted, his voice echoing in the confines of the factory's basement. "Toxins introduced through the mouth."

Robin looked up at him. "What are you talking about?"

As Bane lunged at him, Batman ducked and swung down to Robin's level. "Why is she so desperate to kiss us?" he wondered out loud. "I'm betting her lips carry some kind of poison."

The boy's eyes narrowed with skepticism. "A poison kiss? You have some real issues with women, you know that?"

Robin advanced on his mentor, clearly still under Ivy's influence. "You just couldn't stand that she was about to kiss me."

He shoved Batman.

"Couldn't stand that something might be mine and not yours. Could you?"

Robin shoved him harder still.

Suddenly, Batman was overcome with fury. After all, he'd been pounded enough. Without thinking, he delivered a roundhouse blow, sending Robin smashing into a wall.

Instantly, he was sorry for what he'd done. Heartachingly sorry. Going to Robin's side, he tried to help him up. But the younger man shrugged him off and stood up on his own.

"Ivy's right," he snapped. "I don't need you. I should go solo. I should have my own signal in the sky."

Batman shook his head. "That's ridiculous. You're not ready for something like that."

Robin glared at him. "I'm ready when I *say* I'm ready. And if you don't like it, you can—"

Suddenly, Batman remembered the reason they'd come there in the first place. To get a lead on the villains. He looked around.

But Ivy and Bane were already gone.

Robin regarded him accusingly, as if it were Batman's fault. And maybe it was, the Dark Knight reflected.

Maybe it was.

That's when Commissioner Gordon rushed into the room. "What happened?" he asked. "How'd they get away?"

Unfortunately, Batman didn't have an answer for him. At least, not a good one.

I vy entered Freeze's vault through the snaking passage he had described to her. And just as he had said she would, she discovered the sarcophagus containing Freeze's wife.

The woman was beautiful, no doubt about it. And her beauty wasn't tarnished by her frozen state. If anything, it was enhanced.

For a moment, Ivy considered what to do with the woman. Clearly, she was important to Freeze. But that was the problem, wasn't it?

Looking around, Ivy located the main power switch. Then she turned back to the frozen specimen that had once been a living, breathing person.

"So sorry, Ms. Frigidaire. I'm just not very good with competition," she explained reasonably.

Then she pulled the switch. All over the chamber, status lights flashed red for danger.

Too bad for Freeze's wife there was no one there to see them. No one there to lift a finger to help as her high-tech chrysalis stopped working . . . as she died the death she had been meant to die.

CHAPTER

13

At the Turkish bathhouse on Blossom Street, which Ivy had converted into her personal headquarters, dawn's light streamed through the broken ceiling. The ground, once a floor, was now a rich, thick garden.

Tomato plants and exotic grapevines grew beside and over and through a jungle of cedar saplings and broad-leafed hostas and Japanese maples. There were hundreds of varieties of tree and shrub and ground cover, all coexisting in harmony, all content to be a part of the great intermingling.

Satisfied with the results, Ivy strolled through them into a small anteroom, where Freeze was poring over some kind of freezing engine. Apparently, he had found what he needed to power up his suit again.

And having zapped the walls and the ceiling with his cryo-weapon, he had created a world of ice for himself while he waited for her. Waited, that is, to see her carry out her end of the plan.

Ivy's mouth twitched. All that ice covered what had hours ago been young, thriving plants. She didn't like that, not at all.

But then, she'd killed what Freeze had loved. She could hardly stand on principle now, could she?

"Make yourself right at home," she said sarcastically.

Freeze turned and regarded her. "Where is my wife?" he demanded.

Ivy shrugged. "There was nothing I could do," she lied. "The Bat deactivated her. She's dead."

He was on his feet instantly, eyes blazing with cold fire. "You lie!" he roared, his voice full of pain and fury.

She had never seen him like this. It excited her.

Not hearing the reply he wanted, Freeze lunged for Ivy—but Bane was suddenly there between them, right on schedule. In his rage, Freeze shoved the giant across the room—no easy task.

Bane came back at him with an eye to retaliation, but Ivy stilled him with a gesture. Then she turned to Freeze.

"I'm sorry," she said, lying again. "Really I am. I wish I could have helped her, but I was too late."

Then she reached into her bodice and held out the snow-flake necklace she'd taken from his wife's corpse. Freeze stopped as if mesmerized by it. Slowly, he took the chain in his trembling hand.

His face twisted with savage intent. "Their bones will turn to ice," he promised, his voice a scouring wind out of the north. "Their blood will freeze in my hands."

"Kill them," Ivy agreed. "Of course. But why stop there?" She paused for effect. "Why should only Batman and Robin die while the society that created them goes unpunished?"

Crossing to an ice-covered table, she picked up the frozen bauble of a tiny Gotham City that he'd handed to her at the Flower Ball. Turning it over in her hands, she showed him the blizzard that resulted.

She could feel the intensity of Freeze's glare. The muscles working in his jaw and temples.

"Yes," he hissed, his lips pulling back like a wolf's. "Batman and Robin are just the tip of the iceberg. I will repay the world for sentencing me to a life without the warmth of human comfort. I will blanket the city in end-less winter. First Gotham . . . and then the world."

Ivy looked at him. "Just what I had in mind. Everything dead on earth except us. A chance for Mother Nature to start again with a clean slate." She picked up a frozen blossom. "Plants and flowers are the oldest species on the planet, yet they're defenseless against man." She spoke directly to the flower. "Sorry, hon. This is for science."

Grimacing with sympathy, she crushed the poor thing in her hand. "Behold the dawn of a new age."

Crossing to a canister labeled Project Gilgamesh, Ivy removed a savage, otherworldly plant with hissing fangs. Her favorite, actually.

"What is that?" asked Freeze.

She smiled. "I've created a race of plants with the strength of the deadliest animals. Once you have frozen humankind, my mutant lovelies will overrun the globe. The earth will become a brave, new world of flora without fauna. And we will rule them, you and I. For we will be the only two people left in the world."

Freeze grunted. "Adam and Evil."

So he wasn't entirely enchanted with the prospect. Ivy could accept that. In time, she was certain, he would change his mind.

As she watched, Freeze lifted the bauble, held it in the palm of his hand. His gauntlet glowed blue—and the tiny spires of Gotham froze over. Then he closed his fingers on it and crushed it into frozen pieces.

"You will distract the Bat and the Bird," he told her, "while I prepare to freeze Gotham."

Ivy thought for a moment. "Can't we just ice them along with the rest of the citizenry?"

Freeze shook his head. "No. That is far too merciful. Batman will watch his beloved Gotham perish—just as *my* beloved perished. Then I will kill him with my own hands."

Sounds like a plan, Ivy thought. "As a team, the duncely duo protect each other. But Robin is young. Impetuous. If I could get him alone—"

"One kiss," said Freeze, "and you could lift the mask from his lifeless face. Their secret identities would be revealed."

"Yes," she conceded. "That might be a step in the right direction."

"But how best to bait a bird?" Freeze wondered.

"No problem there," Ivy assured him. "The way to a boy's heart is through his ego. What strapping, young hero could resist his very own . . . signal?"

Her ally nodded coldly. "Inspired, Ms. Ivy."

"You know," she said, placing her hands together, "I'm hungry all of a sudden. I think I'll have some . . . poultry."

Dick stood in the hallway outside Alfred's room alongside Barbara. Dr. Simpson was frowning, deepening the seams in his ruddy, weathered face.

"It's stage one of McGregor's Syndrome," the doctor said soberly. "I'm sorry. All we can do is make him comfortable."

Dick felt numb. Unreal.

He looked past the door to Alfred's room, which was partially open. Bruce was inside, sitting beside Alfred's bed in his black tuxedo. And Alfred was stretched out, looking weaker than the boy had ever seen him.

Dick hadn't known Alfred as long as Bruce had. But that didn't mean he didn't feel the same way about him.

Barbara couldn't speak. For all her courage, all her spunk, she was as floored by the news as Dick was.

Dick bit his lip. "There's got to be *something* we can do to make him better. Something . . ."

Simpson frowned. "Only if you know of a cure, son. To my knowledge, there isn't any."

Dick's eyes lit up as he remembered something.

There is *a cure,* he told himself. *There* is.

"**I** can't do this," said Bruce. "They'll have to find someone else to keynote the dedication."

Alfred looked up at him from his bed. "Nonsense, sir. You *can* do it and you *will*. My being ill doesn't herald the end of the world. There are still duties that must be discharged—both by Bruce Wayne and by his alter ego."

Bruce sighed. Alfred was right, of course. He was always right, always a source of wisdom. The younger man shook his head.

"I've spent my whole life trying to beat back death. I've worked hard at it. But everything I've done, everything I'm capable of doing . . . what's it all for if I can't save *you*?"

Alfred's voice softened. "Everyone dies, Master Bruce. There is no shame in that, no defeat. Victory comes in fighting for what we know is right while we still live."

Bruce looked past Alfred to another time and place. He imagined a younger Alfred reading to him as a boy. He could see the boy's eyes lighting up, fascinated with some adventure, filled with a hopefulness he might never have otherwise known.

Finishing his story, the younger Alfred bade him good night and turned out the light. And the boy bade him good night in turn.

Bruce swallowed and turned to his friend again, tears standing out in his eyes. "I love you, old man. I love you with all my heart."

Alfred sighed. "I know that," he said. "I know also that

I am very proud of you . . . very, very proud. And I love you too . . . son."

They embraced.

It was Alfred who withdrew first. "It's time for you to go," he said. "I'd be a poor manservant indeed if I failed to remind you of that."

Bruce took a tremulous breath, let it out. "You're certain you'll be all right?" he asked.

The butler nodded. "Positive. Nor do I expect you to return immediately after the dedication. After all, that is merely one of the functions you will wish to perform this night."

Bruce smiled. "You know me that well, do you?"

"Better than you know yourself," Alfred told him. Nor was it anything but the truth.

Reluctantly, the younger man left the room. He took his coat from the post at the bottom of the stairs and started for the door.

As he was donning the coat, he saw Dick standing in the foyer. Waiting there for him.

"McGregor's Syndrome," said the boy. "That was what Freeze's wife had."

"Yes," said Bruce, seeing where he was going with this. "Though Alfred's condition is less severe. And yes, Freeze's research says he cured a case like Alfred's. But it doesn't say how."

"I checked the medical database," Dick informed him. "No one else is even close to a cure."

Bruce sighed. "I'm late for the dedication at the observatory. Then I go after Freeze and Ivy. Alone."

His ward's eyes narrowed. "Like hell you do."

Bruce could feel the anger rising in him again. How was it Dick Grayson could press his buttons like no one else in the world?

"Don't push me now," he said.

"Or what?" asked the boy. "No one can capture Ivy but

the big, bad Bat? That's crap, and you know it. You just want her for yourself, don't you? Answer me!"

"Yes!" Bruce blurted. "Yes, I want her so badly I can taste it. That's the whole point. Look at us, Dick. Orphans. Isolated. Obsessed to the exclusion of life, love, family. We're perfect targets for someone like Ivy." He came to a realization even as he said it. "She's done something to us, got us fighting over her somehow."

After Robin's outburst at Freeze's headquarters, the boy seemed to have simmered down. Bruce had believed Dick was in command of his senses again—that he'd managed to overcome Ivy's love dust.

Apparently, he'd been wrong. And it wasn't only Dick who was still laboring under Ivy's influence. Bruce had to admit it was him as well.

"She understands me," Dick said. "For godsakes, she was going to surrender to me."

"She was toying with you," Bruce insisted.

The younger man threw his arms up. "Hail the all-knowing Bruce Wayne! I may not know as much as you, but I know *this*—she loves *me*, not you, and it's driving you crazy. It's why you stopped us from kissing. Because if you can't have her, nobody can."

Bruce shook his head. "That's crazy, Dick. She's clouded your mind. You're not thinking straight."

"Oh," said his ward, "but I *am*. For the first time in a long time, everything's crystal clear. I'm through living in your shadow, Bruce. All that subservient stuff ends here and now."

Having said that, Dick brushed past him, headed for the back door. Bruce stared after him, wondering what to do, what to say. But all he could see when he tried to think was Ivy.

As he attempted to clear his head, the doorbell rang. Abruptly, he realized it wasn't the first time.

He went to answer it. But before he could pull it open,

it swung of its own accord. Or at least it appeared that way until Julie walked in, flushed with anger. There was a limo waiting behind her.

"I've been ringing forever," she huffed. "Where's Alfred?"

Bruce didn't answer. He had to get to Dick, he told himself. He had to reason with the boy before he did something stupid.

But before he could go after him, he heard the roar of a motorbike as it peeled out of the garage. And by that sign, he knew it was too late.

Barbara entered Alfred's room as soon as she saw Bruce depart. But already, the old man in the bed seemed to be slumbering.

"I'm sorry," she said softly. "I was too late."

"Too late for what, dear child?" Alfred asked without opening his eyes.

Barbara looked at him askance. "I thought you were asleep."

"Nonetheless," he said, "you said you were too late. I would like to know of what you were speaking."

She sighed. "I just wanted to take you away from this place. I wanted you to have a chance to live your own life. A man like you doesn't deserve to be a slave, Uncle."

Alfred's eyes opened. They seemed to sparkle, despite his condition. "A slave? Oh no, child."

"Come," she insisted. "You've been a servant, doing things for others you might have done for yourself."

He shook his head. "No. I have been part of something special here—the greatest adventure ever known. I have found purpose in this house, and the family I could never have."

Suddenly, he was hit with a wave of pain. She reached

for him, sat on the bed beside him, and held him until it passed.

"You must do something for me," he said, his voice a little weaker than before. Taking her hand, he put an envelope in it. "Find my brother Wilfred, child. Give him this. I have duties he must fulfill in my stead." He thrust his chin out. "Only family can be trusted."

Barbara looked at the envelope. There was something harder and heavier than a letter in it. "What is it?" she asked.

"It is the sacred trust of two good men, whom I have had the honor of calling son. Take it, child. But I implore you, never open it yourself." Alfred touched her cheek and seemed to look right through her. "You know," he said, "you look so like your mother."

With that, his eyes closed.

She leaned closer to him, consumed with worry. "Uncle Alfred?"

CHAPTER

14

Poison Ivy, hidden in her Pamela Isley persona, stood in the center of the Gotham Observatory and watched the black-tie gala swirl around her.

Her drab outfit and demeanor made her anything but a conversation magnet. But then, that was the way she had planned it.

A storm of camera strobes alerted her to the entrance of someone important—at least by the media's standards. Turning, she saw who it was.

Bruce Wayne—and his airhead actress friend Julie Madison. Ivy snorted as the rich man and his date began greeting the assembled guests. Then she saw her target.

Commissioner Gordon. The same stern-looking civil servant who had warned her about associating with Mr. Freeze, poor chump.

Gordon was in the process of stepping away from the crowd, reaching for a glass of champagne off a waiter's tray. Ivy approached him coyly.

"I've always wondered," she said, "where does that big old bat light come from anyway?"

The commissioner turned to her. But before he could answer, she flipped open a compact and blew a pile of her love dust at him. The tiny puff caught the cop square in the face.

Suddenly, Gordon was stunned. And completely in love. "It's . . . it's on top of police headquarters," he stammered.

Ivy took his arm and led him like a puppy into an alcove. "I'd just love to see it," she told him. "But you probably don't have access to something like that . . . or do you?"

Gordon grinned under his gray moustache. "Why, I'm the commissioner of police." He patted a side pocket. "I have the keys right here."

Out of the corner of her eye, Ivy saw someone headed their way. Cursing inwardly, she turned—and saw it was Bruce Wayne, of all people. As he moved through the crowd, he looked like a man on a desperate quest. And his annoying chippie of a companion didn't seem to be with him.

Then Ivy saw the love dust on the lapel of the rich man's tuxedo, and she understood. A little of what she'd blown at Gordon must've hit Wayne as well. And had the desired effect—or to be more accurate, the effect of desire.

How lovely, she thought. But she didn't have time to capitalize on it. After all, she had to carry out her part of the plan.

Slipping her fingers deftly into Gordon's pocket, she extracted the keys. Then she whirled away from him.

"On second thought," she said, "you're way too old for me."

But as she headed for the exit, she felt a hand close around her arm. Turning, she saw herself staring into the face of Bruce Wayne.

"Dr. Isley," he said. "It was as if I could feel you in the room. You're enchanting. Gorgeous. The most beautiful woman I've ever seen. If you're, um, free . . . this evening . . ."

Suddenly, the Madison woman caught up with him. "Bruce?" she said, her brow creasing with concern. "What in heaven's name are you doing?"

"I think he's asking me on a date," said Ivy. "That is, in an awkward, stammering sort of way."

Madison looked from one of them to the other. Finally, she pulled her date's hand away from Ivy's arm. "I've heard of commitment anxiety," she remarked, "but this is insane. You're not really propositioning another woman right in front of me, are you?"

The billionaire seemed to be having trouble with the concept. Obviously, Ivy thought, with a certain amount of satisfaction, he had other things on his mind.

"Er . . . define 'propositioning,' " he replied.

By then, of course, the press had gotten wind of the confrontation. They were gradually surrounding Ivy, Wayne, and Julie.

"Make a choice," said the starlet, intensely aware of the swarming reporters. "Her or me, Bruce."

The rich man hesitated—but only for a moment. "Well, um . . . her."

Madison was obviously crestfallen. Her lower lip began to tremble. "I get it, Bruce. You're not the marrying kind. You've made your point." She hesitated for a moment, then said, "Good-bye."

And with that, she pushed her way through the crowd. Ivy made a clucking sound as she watched the woman's retreat.

"Physical perfection, charm, and wealth," she said. She turned to Wayne. "All tossed aside for a dowdy little spinster like me? How do you explain your behavior, Mr. Wayne?"

The man seemed puzzled by it himself. "I can't. But perhaps tonight, over a candlelight dinner . . ."

She saw an opening. And having seen it, she went for it with all the viciousness of a Venus's-flytrap.

"Maybe your witless, playboy persona works on your bimbos du jour," she said—just loudly enough for everyone in the room to get an earful. "But I am not the least bit titillated by your attentions, Mr. Wayne. So back off—or I'll have you in court quicker than you can spell sexual harassment."

He looked at her. "Er . . . does that mean dinner's a no?"

People were staring, murmuring to each other. And Wayne was predictably chagrined. Good, thought Ivy. That'd teach him to destroy the ecology with his conglomerate indifference.

Concealing a smile, she pushed past him and headed for the door.

"It's just that I sort of . . . kind of . . . love you," Wayne called after her, his ardor untempered by his embarrassment. "I said I love you," he repeated, this time a little louder.

I'll just bet you do, she mused.

Angry and hurt, Dick gunned his motorcycle down the road that bisected the benighted grounds of the Wayne estate.

The wind in his hair, he popped a wheelie past the pool and the silhouette of the old barn. Then he roared through the woods at the back of the estate, finally emerging at the cliff road beyond.

A right turn would have pointed him toward Gotham's center. He made a left instead, tires screeching as he fishtailed on the roadway and took off in the opposite direction.

Dick leaned into turn after turn on the winding macadam. On his right, past the black expanse of the harbor, he could see the distant lights of downtown sparkling like a scattering of gold and green gems. It was a scattering that seemed to stretch as far as the eye could see.

But then, no matter how far one went, it was tough to get away from Gotham. Didn't people say that all the time?

Hard to get away from this place, very hard. Maybe impossible.

Of course, just then it wasn't the city Dick was trying to get away from. It was Bruce, he realized, scowling. A man who had professed to be his friend. A man he had admired and wanted to emulate.

But what kind of friend hungers after your woman? He demanded an answer with silent fury. What kind of mentor tries to poison the best thing that ever happened to you?

The jealous kind, Dick told himself. The spiteful kind. The kind who can't tolerate the idea that there's something he can't have, despite all his wealth and influence.

The road unfolded before him, zagging this way and then that. To his right, the surf crashed against the rocks; to his left, the trees whipped savagely in the wind off the water.

Why couldn't Bruce just be happy for him, for godsakes? Why couldn't he, of all people on earth, understand how good it felt to be loved again—really *loved*—and to have someone to love in return?

Abruptly, he thought to glance at his watch—to get an idea of how far he'd come. It was farther than he would have imagined. He didn't have much gas left either, not having bothered to fill up before he split. And there weren't any gas stations in this isolated neck of the woods.

If Dick was going to make it back to the manor, he would have to stop and turn around. But he didn't want to go back. Not yet. Not until he knew where he was going with his life.

Catching sight of a clearing with an unobstructed view of Gotham, he pulled over and cut his engine. Then he wheeled his bike over to a tree, leaned it there, and sat down in the untamed grass.

The wind howled around him, echoing the howling in his heart. How could Bruce have become so cruel to him? *How?*

Months earlier, when his family was murdered in an encounter with Two-Face, Dick had been devastated. He hadn't known where to go, whom to turn to. Bruce had taken him under his wing. He had given him a home, a family to replace in some small way the one he'd lost.

And more than that, he had given Dick a purpose. A way to make the bad thing that had happened to him into something good.

Naturally, Dick had been grateful to him. But in all those months, had Bruce ever shown any affection for him? Any real feeling?

Now that the young man thought about it, it was only Alfred from whom he'd gotten any familial vibes—anything approaching compassion or warmth or love. Bruce always seemed so stony, so withdrawn. It was as if he was holding a part of himself back.

No . . .

There had been moments, hadn't there, when Bruce seemed to open up to him? When he treated him like an equal? There had been times when they shared a joke . . . or an appreciation for something . . .

Dick shook his head.

It was hard for him to remember, hard to separate truth from distraction. When he tried to recall the good parts of his stay with Bruce, when he tried to imagine him as something other than a selfish tyrant . . . something happened. And all he could think about was Ivy.

The seductive smell of her. The way her eyes shone, as if with an inner light. The perfection of her, the softness of her skin, and the silken beauty of her hair.

Ivy, who offered him a life of love given and returned. Ivy, for whom he burned with passion as he'd never burned before.

But . . . she was also a criminal, wasn't she? Like the two-faced monster who had put an end to the Flying Graysons? When he thought of her that way, he knew there was no way he could love her.

But he *did* love her, he snarled, holding his fists to his forehead. God help him, he *did*.

Suddenly, Dick saw a way out of his dilemma. He would reform her. He would make her give up her life of crime to be with him. And if Ivy wouldn't do it? If she refused?

He wasn't going to think about that possibility—the same way he hadn't thought about the possibility of falling when he was performing with his family in the big top. He was simply going to do what he had to do.

His mind made up, Dick rose from the grass and straddled his bike. Then he started it up, scooted back onto the road, and headed back in the direction of Wayne Manor.

On the way, it occurred to him there was one other problem with regard to Ivy. How to *find* her.

In Freeze's frozen chamber, the only part of Ivy's Turkish baths in which he felt comfortable, the villain stood and put on his suit.

It was time.

He would grieve for his wife at a later date. Now was his chance to avenge her death, to see to it that Batman didn't go unpunished for his crime.

Freeze gestured, and a legion of Icemen stepped out of the swirling mists, where they had been cooling their heels for the last couple of hours. Of course, they didn't know what he was up to, or they never would have agreed to it. But it was child's play to hire henchmen in this city.

Freeze lifted his freezing engine—the one he'd been working on since his arrival earlier that day—and addressed his thugs. "Bundle up, boys. There's a storm coming."

Then, with his engine of destruction tucked under his arm, he led his doomsday battalion out into the night.

At the same time Freeze was mobilizing his troops, Ivy was carrying out her end of the bargain—following Bane up a poorly lit stairway.

Commissioner Gordon's key had worked like a charm, giving them access to a little-used set of stairs leading to the roof of the police headquarters building. It was a good thing, too. If it *hadn't* worked, she might have had to enchant every officer in the place with her love dust—and then who would have protected the streets of Gotham?

She laughed at her little conceit. If all went well, not even an army of cops would be able to save this city and its people. And so far, everything was going well indeed.

On the stairs up ahead of her, Bane came to a door. Grasping the doorknob, he swung it open. Strong as he was, it was torn halfway off its hinges, exposing them to a spill of starlight. Then he stood aside and let Ivy lead the way up onto the roof.

She was no longer wearing the appearance of the woman she used to be—the plain-looking wallflower who'd been overlooked much too long. Poison Ivy was herself again, in all her emerald glory.

At the far end of the roof, the Bat-Signal stood dormant. *But not for long*, she thought. She pointed to it.

"Let there be light," she said.

That was Bane's cue. Walking over to the signal, the Venom-powered giant tore it from its shackles and carried it back to the stairs.

Ivy followed, a smile on her full, green lips. Even the weather appeared to be cooperating with her. There was a line of gray cumulus clouds moving in from the harbor already. If the weatherman could be believed, it would arrive just when she needed it.

Her smile widened. Pretty soon, it would be tough to be a weatherman around here. But then, it would be tough to be *anyone* around here.

CHAPTER

15

Barbara stood over her uncle and swallowed back her tears.

His face was partially masked by a breathing apparatus, a tube going from his arm to an intravenous bag suspended above him. Under his pajamas, a sensor had been attached to his chest over his heart.

At the moment, the electrocardiogram machine showed the rise and fall of a relatively normal heartbeat. But with the disease eating away at him, how long could that be expected to go on?

Sighing heavily, Barbara pulled her uncle's bedclothes up a little higher. It hadn't taken the doctor long to get the necessary equipment for Alfred to be placed on life support. She supposed it was one of the benefits of Bruce Wayne's being the wealthiest man in Gotham. When his name was mentioned, people jumped.

Still, it had been a frightening experience. All at once, Uncle Alfred's pulse had become terribly weak, his breathing so shallow as to be almost undetectable. Her first impression was that he had died.

Perhaps in a sense, she reflected, he *had*. Without the machines taking over the functions his body should have been performing, without the intervention of technology, they'd likely have been saying last rites over him now.

And where were his friends Bruce and Dick? Why had she been the only one home in Uncle Alfred's time of need?

Barbara made her way to her room, feeling drained and battered, lost in grief and bitterness. It had been so long since she'd seen her uncle. So long since she'd made herself a promise to free him from his servitude. To lose him now . . .

Plopping herself down on the bed, she remembered the envelope Uncle Alfred had given her. It was on the antique commode beside her bed, where she'd put it while the medical people were doing their job.

Reaching for it, she held the envelope up to the lamp that stood on the commode. Inspected it. Turned it over in her hands.

What was inside it? she wondered. Why had her uncle asked her never to open it? Didn't he know she couldn't resist anything and everything that was forbidden to her?

Biting her lip, she wrestled with her dilemma for a moment. Then she gave in to her curiosity and opened the envelope.

There was a disc inside. A silver compact disc. "Only family can be trusted," she echoed softly.

Well, *she* was family, wasn't she? Perhaps Alfred hadn't given her his genes, but he'd given her his heart.

Crossing the room, she slid the disc into the computer Bruce Wayne had been good enough to provide her with. Then she tried to access the information contained in it.

"Access denied," said the computer.

Barbara sat down and began hacking the disc, trying to crack the code. Fortunately, she was nearly as good with computers as she was with motorbikes. It would only be a matter of time before she got inside.

Slumped against the door frame, Bruce peered into Alfred's room from the hallway outside. He was terribly ashamed of himself.

And terribly confused.

When had this happened? he wondered. When had his old butler, who had seemed so stable and alert just a few hours ago, sunk so far that he needed a web of supports to keep him alive?

Where was Dick? And Barbara?

Making his way through the house and up the stairs, Bruce found his ward's door open—and his room empty. Wherever Dick had gone, it seemed he still hadn't come back.

The girl's door, on the other hand, was closed. He knocked hopefully.

"Barbara?" he called. "Are you in there?"

A moment later, the door opened. The girl's eyes were red-rimmed, but she seemed calm enough. In the background, her computer was on.

"What happened?" he asked weakly.

She knew just what he meant. She told him how Alfred's condition had worsened suddenly. How she'd called the doctor, and how the doctor had set up the life supports.

And she told him the prognosis. It wasn't good.

Bruce looked at her. "Are you all right?" he asked.

Barbara shrugged. "As well as can be expected."

It was the same thing Alfred had said when Bruce asked him about his health. He nodded.

"If you need me, just holler."

"I'll do that," she promised.

It seemed she wanted to be alone—just as much as he wanted not to be. But he would allow her whatever she wished.

As he walked back down the stairs, he tore away the tie to his tuxedo. If he was going to be alone, he told himself, he'd be alone in the place he felt most comfortable: the Batcave.

It took him only moments to go down there and seat himself in front of the main computer console. But before long, he wasn't looking at the console anymore or the screens that loomed above it. He was staring into the darkness, the shadows . . .

. . . where he saw a younger Alfred with a Bruce in his early twenties. The two of them were working on the prototype for the original Batsuit.

Was it his imagination . . . or had Alfred been even more determined than he was to get it right? To optimize the suit's efficiency without mitigating the terror it would inspire?

The memory faded. Bruce smiled to himself. For all its uncertainty, for all the peril inherent in the undertaking, those had been happy times. For both of them, he believed.

Lately, he'd had to do some tinkering without his lifelong friend. After all, the threat of Freeze didn't seem eager to go away—and the Batmobile wasn't equipped for every need Bruce could envision. As a result, he'd stepped up the pace on the new vehicles.

At this stage of the game, he was perfectly capable of building such things on his own. Still, he craved Alfred's insights and expertise . . . and his plain, old-fashioned common sense.

And not just when it came to machines.

"Alfred," he sighed, "I could use your help right now."

"Right here, sir," said a familiar voice.

Bruce whirled, stunned. Before his eyes, a monitor flickered into life. The words COMPUTER SIMULATION flashed a couple of times under a digitized image of Alfred.

"I anticipated a moment might arrive," said the image,

"where I became incapacitated. As a precaution against such a circumstance, I programmed my brain algorithms into the Batcomputer and created a virtual simulation—the one you see before you."

Bruce stared for a moment. Then he shook his head in admiration of the older man's genius.

"It's good to see you," he told the Alfred image.

"What seems to be the problem?" it asked, as if it were Alfred himself.

Bruce grunted softly. "You are."

The image seemed to stare at him for a moment. "Surely, I am not the only cause of your distress."

It was true—there was another one. "Women," Bruce replied.

The Alfred program seemed to pause. "That does not compute, sir. Would you like to rephrase your reply?"

The billionaire mulled it over. It didn't compute for him either, he realized. That was the problem.

"First," he said, thinking out loud, "Poison Ivy had an intoxicating effect on both Dick and me. Tonight my feelings spread to someone else."

"Specify, please," said Computer Alfred.

"Pamela Isley. I was so attracted to her I couldn't reason clearly. I still can't." He bit his lip. "She used to work for Wayne Enterprises. Find a file for me, will you?"

"Coming on-line now, sir."

A spinning picture of Isley appeared on the monitor. "What was her area of research?" Bruce asked.

Study and report titles scrolled up beside the woman's image. "Advanced botany," Alfred responded. "DNA splicing. Recombinant animal plant patterns. Pheromone extraction . . ."

Bruce held up his hand—as if he expected the computer to see it and stop. "Pheromones?" he echoed.

"Glandular secretions from animals," Alfred expanded. "Scents that create powerful emotions. Fear. Rage . . ."

"Passion," said Bruce. He was beginning to understand. "Find the photo of Ivy after the Flower Ball."

A spinning Ivy appeared beside the spinning Isley.

"Deconstruct and resolve, Alfred."

Schematics of various features—finger and retina prints, height, weight, and so on—were highlighted, analyzed, and compared. Each and every one of them matched perfectly.

Bruce grunted softly. "Amazing what a good wig and contact lenses can do. And I thought Clark Kent got away with murder wearing just those glasses."

He knew now why he'd acted like such a schoolboy at the reception earlier. And why his brain felt so muddled now. Somehow, he must've caught a whiff of Ivy's phero-mone-powered influence—though she had delivered it in the guise of Pamela Isley.

Suddenly, alert panels began flashing on the console. Alarms sounded all over the Batcave.

"What is it?" asked Bruce.

"Apparently," said Alfred, "someone has stolen the Bat-Signal."

Barbara peeked out through the crack in her door. Bruce was gone. Where, she didn't know. Maybe out for a walk in the garden.

She hated having been so short with him. After all, he had to be hurting too. If Dick was right, Uncle Afred had been like family to him.

But she was close to hacking her way into the contents of her uncle's disc. So close she could *feel* it.

Sitting down at her computer again, Barbara tried an-other password—the one she'd been on the verge of key-ing in when Bruce had knocked on her door. It was her mother's name.

M-A-R-G-A-R-E-T.

"Access denied," said the computer.

The girl frowned. She had been so certain her mother would have something to do with it. After all, Margaret Clark still had a place of honor on Alfred's bureau.

Wait a second . . . how had it been inscribed? Not from "Margaret." From . . .

Barbara typed in three letters. *P-E-G.*

"Access code accepted," the computer informed her.

Pay dirt.

Barbara leaned back in her chair. "This had better be one whopper of a secret," she said to herself. Then she hit the required key and the monitor unveiled the contents of the disc.

She scanned them, her eyes growing ever wider. "Oh my God," she whispered. And then again: "Oh my God."

Freeze screeched his truck to a stop. Behind him, all his cronies' trucks stopped as well.

He turned to Bane, who was sitting beside him, only his eyes visible through the slits of his leather mask. And even those were the eyes of an animal, not a man.

"No matter what they tell you," Freeze said, "it's the size of your gun that counts."

Bane's bloodshot eyes narrowed in their slits, but he didn't respond otherwise. More than likely, thought Freeze, the man in the mask had no idea what he was talking about.

Not that it mattered. He was a tool, nothing more. When he was no longer useful, Freeze would discard him.

Looking up, the villain saw the giant telescope of the Gotham Observatory aimed into the night. He waited seventeen seconds until the appointed moment arrived. Then he scrutinized the sky above the telescope.

Suddenly, a beam of light stabbed the night, piercing a

nest of gathering storm clouds. A symbol appeared in the midst of those clouds. The emblem of a bat with its wings outstretched.

The Bat-Signal.

Then something happened. The familiar beacon turned blood red and the shape within it changed from bat to bird. Before long, it was the Robin signal that was shining over Gotham.

Freeze laughed his empty laugh. So far, it seemed, Ivy had her part down cold. Now it was up to him.

As soon as Dick entered the house, he knew something was wrong. It was just too quiet, too somber in the big, echoing mansion. And he had an awful feeling why that might be.

When he got to Alfred's room, his feelings were confirmed. For a moment, he just stood there, stunned. Then he went inside.

Alfred didn't acknowledge him. He couldn't. He was in some kind of coma, kept alive by the grace of the machines around him.

The boy became angry at himself. The old man had been good to him. He should have been there for Alfred, as Alfred had been there for *him*.

Then he realized there was nothing he could have done. Alfred was dying. Bruce had said so. This was only the inevitable coming to pass.

Checking to make sure the old man wasn't in need of anything, Dick left him and made his way to the grandfather clock situated in the library. Turning the hands to 10:47—the exact time of Bruce's parents' death—he heard the hidden door unlock.

He could have gone upstairs to look for Barbara instead. But right now, he wanted to see Bruce—and just as he had known something was wrong as soon as he entered the house, he knew now that Bruce was in his sanctum.

Swinging the clock aside, Dick entered the Batcave. A moment later, the clock swung back into place behind him and he descended the stairs.

Bruce was sitting in front of the computers. He looked up as Dick came down the steps. "You've seen him?" he asked softly.

The younger man looked at him. "What happened?"

Bruce explained, relaying the information he had gotten from Barbara. "And I wasn't here. I was off at that dedication."

Dick frowned. "Don't beat yourself up. I wasn't here either." By then, he was close enough to get a glimpse of what was on the screen.

It was Alfred. But how . . . ?

"A computer simulation," Bruce told him. "Alfred programmed it into the computer, knowing he was dying."

"And that we would still need him," Dick observed, awed by the man's sense of duty.

Bruce nodded. "Something like that."

"Good evening, Master Dick," said Alfred's image.

"Hi, Al," he replied hesitantly.

The image flinched ever so slightly—just the way the real Alfred would have. *Amazing*, Dick thought. *Absolutely amazing.*

"I've figured a few things out," said Bruce. "With Alfred's help, of course. It turns out—"

"Sir," Alfred's image announced, "I believe we have located the Bat-Signal—or a reasonable facsimile thereof."

A moment later, the program accessed one of the mansion's external cameras and replaced the butler's image with another one. But it wasn't the Bat-Signal Dick saw.

It was something else entirely.

CHAPTER

16

Bruce stared at the giant computer screen. What he saw made him gape. It was a signal, all right, glowing against the underbelly of a cloud. But it wasn't a black bat emblazoned on a field of gold.

It was a black bird on a field of blood red.

Bruce scowled—but Dick seemed to be enjoying it. "That's no Bat-Signal," he observed. "It's a birdcall." Then he headed for his costume vault.

"Where are you going?" the older man asked.

Dick disappeared inside. "I'm suiting up. In case you hadn't noticed, that signal was meant for me."

Bruce pounded on the wall of the costume vault. "For godsakes, Dick, her name is Pamela Isley. I saw her talking to Commissioner Gordon."

"No law against that," Dick noted from inside the vault.

"She must have stolen his keys," the billionaire realized. "Altered the signal to suit her plans."

Dressed except for his mask, Robin emerged from the vault and shot him a prideful look. "And she did it all for me, Bruce. For *me*."

He shook his head. "No, Dick. She just wants you to think she did."

His protégé pulled on his mask and walked past him. Clearly, he was headed for his bike.

"Listen to me," Bruce called after him, his voice echoing in the cavern. "She's infected us with some kind of pheromone extract. It makes her the focus of our desires. Muddles our senses—"

Robin stopped and looked back at him. "Uh-huh. I get it. I'm under some kind of magic spell. Yeah, right."

"She wants to kill you," the older man told him.

His ward was clearly unconvinced. "You'd say anything to keep me away from her. To keep her for yourself."

There was anger in his voice. And resentment. And a slew of other emotions Bruce couldn't identify.

He saw he wasn't getting anywhere this way. He would need another tack—one that would open Dick's eyes to the truth. One that would speak to him in his own language.

Then it came to him.

Bruce pointed to the boy, fixing him to the spot. "You once told me being part of a team means trusting your partner. You said counting on someone else is sometimes the only way to win. You remember?"

Dick didn't answer. But for the first time since they met Poison Ivy, Bruce felt as if he might be getting through to him.

"You weren't just talking about being partners," the older man went on. "You were talking about being a family. Well, one member of our family is dying upstairs." He could feel a rush of emotion, of determination. "I'm not going to lose everyone I've ever loved—not if I can help it. So I'm asking you now . . . friend . . ."

No. Not just that.

". . . partner . . ."

Dick's eyes lit up a little at the notion. Still, that wasn't all Bruce wanted to say. There was more.

But it wasn't easy to say the word. It wasn't easy to

make himself vulnerable in a world that had proven its cruelty to him at every turn.

But he did it anyway. For Dick's sake.

". . . brother . . ."

The boy swallowed. But then, he had to know how hard it had been for his mentor to open up like that.

". . . will you trust me?" asked Bruce.

The Batcave echoed: *. . . trust me . . . trust me . . . trust me . . .*

In the vast silence that followed, he awaited Dick's answer.

Freeze smashed open the door to the observatory. Bane was right behind him, a satchel in his hand.

Two men turned to look down at them from the tower platform, eyes wide with apprehension. Scientists, from the look of them. Having been one, Freeze knew the type. No doubt, they had been cooing over their prize telescope amid the debris from its dedication party, congratulating themselves on their good fortune.

Which was about to end.

"Hi," said Freeze. "Sorry about the door." He looked around, feigning interest. "Am I too late for the party?"

According to plan, Bane began pulling charges from his satchel and setting them around the room.

One of the scientists turned to the other and jerked a thumb in Freeze's direction. "Who's *this* nutball?"

Freeze took out his gun and fired a cryonic blast at the man, turning him to ice. He froze in mid-scream.

"That's *Mr.* Nutball to you," the villain told him. He tilted his head appraisingly. "You'd make a good bookend, but you're only half a set." He turned to the other scientist. "You. Go like *this*."

Freeze pantomimed the first scientist's frozen expression of terror for the benefit of the second one. Too frightened to resist, the man imitated Freeze's movements.

"No," said the villain. "Move your hands up. Higher . . . stop. Now a hint more fear. Excellent."

Satisfied, Freeze fired another cryonic blast, freezing the second scientist in the same position as the first one. "A matched pair," he said. "Sometimes I exceed even my wildest expectations."

That done, he raised his eyes to the mighty telescope and smiled. It would do the job nicely. *More* than nicely. Freeze was reminded of the inmate's remark back in Arkham.

He looked at Bane. "If revenge is a dish best served cold, then put on your Sunday finest, my friend. It's time for a feast."

Barbara descended into the Batcave, eyes wide with awe. It was dark, dormant. She could hear a distant hiss and flitter of movement, echoing from wall to wall, but no hint of another human being.

Abruptly, the automatic activation sequence engaged. Ambient lights blinked on. Great computers flickered to life.

At the other side of the cavern, a giant pedestal began to rise in a cloud of steam. It was the Batmobile, she realized. It had to be.

Skin crawling, throat dry, she crossed to the main computer console. Touched it almost reverently. And was startled to see her uncle's face appear on the central monitor.

"Uncle . . . Alfred?" she stammered.

Her uncle's image smiled. "In spirit only, I'm afraid."

Barbara realized then what was going on. It was a computer program, designed to somehow simulate her uncle's personality—and perhaps his accumulated knowledge as well.

She glanced at the flanking monitors. The one on the left showed her a signal in the cloudy night sky. *Like the Bat-Signal,* she thought, *but with some significant differences.*

"The Robin signal," Barbara realized.

"So it would seem," the image of her uncle confirmed.

Then she turned to the flanking monitor on her right. There were actually two images there, both of them revolving slowly. One was a woman, no one she knew. The other fit the description of Poison Ivy.

The mystery woman who had appeared at the Flower Ball. And who was believed to have helped Mr. Freeze spring himself from Arkham Asylum.

One look at her told Barbara the woman was dangerous—in a way Batman and Robin might not be prepared for. She glanced at the Robin signal again, then turned back to the picture of Ivy.

Dangerous indeed. She didn't know all the details—but then, she didn't have to. "The boys need help," she murmured.

Alfred's computer image smiled at her in a decidedly conspiratorial way—as if it had come to that conclusion itself some time ago. "Your mother would be proud," it told her.

As Barbara watched, the images on the flanking screens changed, yielding to identical sets of costume schematics. Turning three-dimensional, the schematics began to turn.

"Forgive my being personal," Alfred's image said, "but I must know your measurements, my dear."

"My . . . measurements?" she repeated. "Whatever for?"

And then, all at once, she realized what her uncle's program was up to.

As Robin traced the Bird-Signal to its source, he screeched around a corner and turned onto Blossom Street, in what had once been Gotham City's thriving theater district.

Now the street was dark, most of the businesses boarded up and abandoned. Except for one place, halfway down the block. It didn't seem to be a business, but it was certainly teeming with life.

The *vegetable* variety, Robin mused.

The facade of the building was completely overgrown with vines and creepers and exotic blossoms. As he rode closer, he saw that it had been a Turkish bathhouse at one time. Now it was something else—a jungle, lush, inviting, and mysterious. *Not unlike Ivy herself,* he reflected.

A giant red symbol of a bird was chained to the door. There was a spotlight gleaming behind it, spearing the underside of the clouds with what looked like a bloody wound.

Coasting to a halt, Robin got off his bike and kicked its stand out. As he approached the entrance—really nothing more than an opening in the overgrowth—he saw the Bird-Signal go out.

Obviously, it was no longer needed. He was here, wasn't he?

With more curiosity than caution, he entered the building. It was lush and mysterious inside, too. Giant floral fans spun dangling from the ceiling. Leaf curtains undulated in the breeze created by his entrance. Full, ripe fruits seemed ready to burst with the promise of pleasure.

And Poison Ivy lounged on a giant bed of buds in the middle of it all, clearly the mistress of this floral domain. In recognition of Robin's appearance, she touched the buds on which she rested. They blossomed instantly, transforming themselves into a riot of color.

Robin smiled. He felt good in Ivy's presence, intoxicated with her beauty. He came a little closer.

"Is your thumb the only part of you that's green?" he asked.

The green woman smiled back at him. "You'll just have to find out." She extended her hand to him.

Stepping out of the shadows, he took it.

At Gotham Tower, perched alongside the scientists on a platform overlooking the observatory floor, Freeze began the intricate process of attaching his powerful icing engine to the massive telescope.

At the same time, Bane laid his explosive charges on the floor below. Unlike Freeze's task, it didn't take long. When he was done, he climbed up the tower to stand by Freeze.

Even when he was a simple molecular biologist, Freeze had hated to have people hover over him as he worked. Silent people, especially. Becoming a creature of the cold hadn't changed him in that respect.

He looked up at Bane. "Big family?"

Bane just stared at him through the slits in his mask.

"Like pets?"

Still no answer. Just that stare.

"Don't talk much, do you?"

Bane remained silent. As always.

Just as well, thought Freeze. The fellow didn't look like he'd have a whole lot to say.

Turning back to his work, the villain completed his preparations and engaged the engine. Suddenly, the entire platform was washed in a blue wave of freezing cryonic energy.

Bane leaped down to avoid it. But Freeze basked in it.

At least for a while. Then, with a wink at the scientists, he climbed down and looked out one of the windows in the place.

From his vantage point, he watched a wave of blue-white ice spread from the telescope to the outside of the building, and then descend along its flanks. Before long, the wave had encased the edifice, turning it into an icy fortress. But it wasn't done there.

The ice wave spread even farther, whitening the banks of the Gotham River, turning them into snow cliffs. And after that, the river itself came under its influence. In a matter of seconds, it had frozen solid.

Freeze considered the fruits of his labor and nodded approvingly. It was just as he'd pictured it.

In the midst of her private jungle, Poison Ivy sat on her bed of many-colored buds and drew Robin down beside her, until their faces were only a few small inches apart.

"I'm glad you came," she murmured. "I can't breathe without you."

"I want us to be together," the boy said earnestly, even passionately. "But I need to know you're serious about turning over a new leaf."

"You have my word," she told him.

"I need a sign."

"How about dangerous curves?" she suggested.

"A sign of *trust*," he said. "Tell me your plan."

Ivy smiled. "Kiss me and I'll tell you."

"Tell me and I'll kiss you," Robin whispered.

What could it hurt? she thought. He wasn't going to live to tell about it anyway. "Freeze has turned the new telescope into a freezing gun. He's going to turn Gotham City into an ice cube."

Robin recoiled. "I've got to stop him."

Ivy pulled him back. "One kiss, my love. For luck."

The boy hesitated for a moment—but only for a moment. Then he gave in to her charms.

They kissed, eagerly and irrevocably.

Then Ivy withdrew and stroked his cheek with her fingertips. "Bad luck, I'm afraid. It's time to die, little bird."

Robin looked at her, obviously as confused as a little bird could be. "What do you mean?"

"You should have heeded your pointy-eared pal," she told him. "These lips of mine can be murder."

Understanding began to dawn on his flawless, young face. "Then . . . you never loved me?" he asked, with almost childish innocence.

"Loved you?" she echoed, making it sound like the most ridiculous thing she'd ever heard of. "I *loathe* you. I loathe your bipedal arrogance, your so-called animal superiority. My only joy is knowing that even now my poison kiss is sucking the life from your apelike face."

"I'll resist saying I told you so," said someone in the shadows—someone Ivy hadn't noticed until now. The hairs rose on the back of her neck as she saw Batman move into the light.

"You're too late," she spat. "Say bye-bye, Birdie."

Robin chuckled—not exactly the reaction she would've expected from a dying man. "Sorry to disappoint you," he told her, "but rubber lips are immune to your charms."

With that, he peeled a thin rubber coating from his mouth. Ivy stared at it in dismay.

"Robin and I found the cure to your evil spell," Batman noted. "And that's teamwork."

Ivy felt a red-hot fury building inside her. She let it out in a long, bloodcurdling scream. Then she shoved Robin into the lily pool beside them, where predatory vines reached out and enveloped him.

Before Batman could come to his aid, she had other

vines grab the Dark Knight by the ankles and wrench him upside down. Then her children began to squeeze the life out of Bat and Bird.

"Sorry, boys," she said, "but my vines have a little crush on you." Then she leaped from lily pad to lily pad, headed for the exit. "Gotta run. So many people to kill, so little time."

But before she could get away, the skylight overhead seemed to implode, filling the room with moonlight—and a figure came flipping down from above. Judging by the long cape, the sleek eye mask, and the molded rubber, Ivy thought she was dealing with another Batman.

Then she realized that wasn't the case at all. This Batman was very definitely a woman.

The feminine curves were a giveaway. And if Ivy still weren't sure, a look at the thigh-length boots and heels would have convinced her.

"Who are you?" the villainess asked.

"I'm Batgirl," the woman told her, her eyes hard and determined through the eye slits of her cowl. "And you're about to become compost."

"Not likely," Ivy replied.

Nonetheless, the newcomer turned out to be a lot more formidable than she looked. She was strong, agile, and she had a command of the martial arts Pamela Isley could only have dreamed about.

But Ivy had some tricks of her own—an entire jungle of them, in fact. With a gesture, she sent a mess of snake-like vines darting at her adversary. Unfortunately, the woman eluded them and landed a couple of hammerlike blows to Ivy's jaw.

The villainess staggered, dazed. Instantly, the jungle closed around her, protecting her from further punishment.

"Using feminine wiles to get what you want," the new-comer snapped. "Trading on your looks. Exploiting men's weakness for sex. Read a book, sister. That passive-aggressive crap went out twenty years ago. Chicks like you give women a bad name."

Off to the side, Batman was slashing through the vines that held him captive, using something bat-shaped and razor-edged. And in the lily pond, Robin was struggling to free himself.

It was only a matter of time before both of them succeeded. Ivy knew that. And she didn't want to be here when it happened.

Clenching her jaw, she let Batgirl have it with every weapon in her arsenal. The intruder was assaulted with a barrage of nuts and berries, fruits and vegetables. It pushed her back, back, until she was slumped against the wall.

Only when Ivy was satisfied all the fight had been taken out of her did she come forward and lord it over the newcomer. "As I told Lady Freeze when I pulled her plug, this is a one-woman show."

Suddenly, Batgirl was on her feet, not nearly as battered as she'd let on. "I don't *think* so," she said.

Ignoring the effects of the barrage with which Ivy had hit her, Barbara grabbed Ivy's hair and brought her knee up into Ivy's face. The woman crumpled suddenly, bereft of consciousness.

Taking a set of handcuffs from her Utility Belt, Barbara shackled the green woman. Then she saw something big and black drop from the ceiling and she whirled.

It was Batman. Obviously, he'd cut himself free.

A moment later, Robin emerged from the pool, dripping water all over the vegetation-covered floor. Like his partner, he had a distinct look of incredulity on his face.

"And you are?" asked Batman.

"Batgirl," she said. It was the name she'd given Ivy without thinking.

"That's not very politically correct," Robin told her. "How about Batwoman? Or Batperson?"

Batman's eyes narrowed. Clearly, he didn't trust her. Even though she'd taken out Ivy, she was an unknown quantity.

Frowning, she did the only thing she could do to earn his trust. She slipped off her cowl.

"It's me," she said. "Barbara. I found the cave."

The two of them looked at her. Then they looked at each other.

"We've gotta get those locks changed," said Robin.

"She knows who we are," Batman pointed out.

His sidekick nodded. "I guess we'll have to kill her."

For a moment, Barbara was afraid they meant it. But they didn't lift a hand against her. And Robin actually smiled.

"Kill her later," Batman said at last. "Right now, we've got work to do."

He and Robin made their way out of the baths. And Barbara—no, Batgirl—was right behind them.

CHAPTER

17

Standing on the floor-level telescope platform at the Gotham Observatory, Freeze gripped the giant telescope, gazed into its viewfinder, and laughed at the sound of approaching sirens.

"One Adam-twelve, one Adam-twelve, see the mad scientist with the freezing ray. Respond with caution if you know what's good for you."

A squad of cruisers screamed up the avenue toward the observatory, their bubble lights flashing. "I guess they don't know what's good for them," said Freeze. "Cops on the rocks, anyone?"

With that, he fired a giant blue beam of cryonic energy at the street below. Suddenly, the cop cars became skidding, screeching cubes of ice, smashing into each other—and ultimately exploding into pyres of raging flames.

"Police are so hot-tempered these days," Freeze remarked. He turned to glance at his muscle-bound accomplice. "Don't you agree, Mr. Bane?"

Bane didn't answer. *Nothing new there*, thought Freeze.

Then a distant flurry of activity caught his eye. He trained the telescope on it and took another look through the viewfinder.

It was Batman, behind the wheel of a modified white Batmobile on rocket skis, blazing a trail over the frozen river. Also his pitiful companion, Robin, guiding a sleek, one-man iceboat over the ice.

And a third person, also dressed in the cowl and cape of Batman. But this one was a woman, it seemed to him. And she was driving some kind of single-bladed, rocket-powered snowcycle.

Very nice, Freeze mused. *A regular Batforce*. Obviously, Ivy had failed to unmask the crime fighters and keep her part of the bargain.

"No matter," he said out loud. "The Bat and the Bird are mine at last." He shook a fist at Batman. "Watch as your beloved Gotham freezes," he bellowed. "And prepare to die—because you're next!"

Pointing the telescope downtown, Freeze zeroed in on a particular street and fired. Then he observed the results through the viewfinder.

He could still see folks walking their dogs, drinking canned beverages on stoops, kissing in the shadows of alley walls. He could still see mailboxes, lampposts, the pavement itself. Except now, it was all flash-frozen, encased in a thick, glistening coat of ice.

Lovely, thought Freeze. *Just lovely.*

Then he turned his weapon on his crime-fighting enemies again and spoke into his built-in radio hookup. After all, he was prepared for this eventuality. In fact, he'd looked forward to it.

"The Bat-talion approaches," he snarled. "Icemen—attack!"

Down below, his drill truck burst through the mists that had accumulated by the riverbanks. Then it blasted down the frozen waterway on sharp, silver blades. Two pairs of Icemen hung from tail lines on skis, machine guns blazing like torches in the night.

Freeze didn't normally like heat very much. But in this case, he would make an exception.

Batgirl saw Freeze's truck coming at them from upriver. She turned to Batman for instructions.

"Attack plan Alpha," he said, speaking into his radio. Suddenly, he peeled off to the left.

"Alpha," Robin confirmed. "Roger." He peeled right.

"Alpha," Batgirl repeated. "Got it." Then she realized she was at a bit of a disadvantage. "What's attack plan Alpha?"

She heard a chuckle over the radio. "Divide and conquer," Robin explained.

He was veering downriver as he said it. A pair of Icemen noticed and swept out alongside the drill truck, heading toward Robin's billowing craft with their guns firing.

Batgirl wanted to help him. Unfortunately, she was about to have her hands full. A second pair of skiing Icemen were whipping around in her direction, their guns spitting bullets into the ice around her.

And a set of rocket launchers, side-mounted onto the truck, were firing at Batman's craft, blowing holes in the ice. It looked like each of them was on his or her own.

Robin spared only a moment to watch Batman maneuver his vehicle through the Icemen's barrage. Somehow, his mentor managed to swerve around the sudden, steaming holes in the icy river. Then, gunning his turbos, Batman headed straight for Freeze's truck.

At the same time, the two Icemen bearing down on Robin released their tethers and used their momentum to converge on his Batsled. They came straight at him, guns blazing.

"Tack," said Robin.

Pulling on his tiller, he brought his craft sharply around—taking himself out of the path of the two skiers. The Icemen collided, then slid past him on the ice.

Boy, he thought, as he left the skiers in his wake. *I hope for Freeze's sake he buys these guys by the dozen.*

Batgirl frowned. Freeze's skiers were closing fast with her Batblade. Remembering Batman's instructions, she hit a key and a status panel displayed a menu of her vehicle's special functions.

"Nice extras package," Batgirl muttered, seeing it now for the first time.

She thought for a moment, then selected a setting called "ice cutter." Suddenly, the Batblade's scythe peeled back, revealing a much sharper blade beneath it.

Applying the same skills that won her all those motor-cycle races, Batgirl spun and side-skidded, her blade sending a cascade of frozen ice into the faces of the oncoming Icemen. Unable to hang on to their tow ropes under the onslaught, the villains were driven backward in helpless somersaults across the surface of the frozen river.

Batgirl had a new appreciation for her vehicle as she brought it out of its side skid. "Now, that's what I call a close shave."

In the vehicle Robin had already nicknamed the Bathammer, Batman was shooting for the center of the frozen river, heading straight for Freeze's truck. Its side guns blazed at him.

Clenching his jaw, the Dark Knight hit a control stud—sending two torpedoes shooting out of the Bathammer's chassis. They hit the frigid surface directly in front of Freeze's truck and exploded, sending chunks of ice flying in every direction.

The driver of the truck must have seen the hole in the ice created by the blast, but he was unable to swerve in time. The truck hit the steaming pool, tilted up nose first, and began to sink into the icy waters.

As Batman whipped past the vehicle, he glanced out his window to assure himself that Freeze's henchmen were able to crawl to safety. From the looks of things, they'd be fine.

"Don't sink and drive," he breathed.

Then he went on to his next objective—that being Gotham Observatory. As Freeze's beams bathed the city, the Bathammer fired its turbos and closed in on the beams' source.

Freeze cursed. His Icemen had barely even slowed Batman down, and the crime fighter's sidekicks were unscathed as well. He tilted the telescope down until he had them in his sights.

"Not so fast," he said. "Time you cooled your heels."

Then he fired.

The freezing ray hit the frozen channel in front of the Bat-trio and created a wall of rock-hard ice, effectively blocking the river from one bank to the other. Freeze grunted with satisfaction.

"Let them plow their way through that," he grated.

The words were barely out of his mouth before Batman's vehicle went into some kind of overdrive and blew a hole right through the frozen barrier. Freeze flinched, as if he'd felt the impact himself.

The other two Batvehicles negotiated the wall their own way—by shooting up the face of it and sailing over. They hit the ice on the other side without missing a beat and whipped in alongside the speeding Batman.

Freeze cursed again, this time more volubly. His targets were too close to the observatory building now to be seen, much less fired at. He turned to a monitor, which showed him the Bat-team making its way up the giant cliffs at the tower's base.

He turned to his own sidekick. The giant in the leather mask stood by patiently, awaiting his orders as Poison Ivy had instructed.

"Mr. Bane," said Freeze, "I'll finish off the city. You, as they say in show business, are on. Take the boys and kill those meddling kids." He leaned closer to the muscle-bound Bane, so there would be no mistake. "But bring the Bat to *me*."

As Batgirl scaled Freeze's ice cliffs, using the spikes and ropes she'd found stored in her Batblade, she glanced at her newfound allies. If someone had told her a week ago that she'd be working with Batman and Robin, she'd have called them crazy.

Yet here she was.

"We have eleven minutes to stop Freeze and thaw the city," said Batman, shouting to be heard over the howl of the wind.

Batgirl wasn't sure how he knew that. On the other hand, she wasn't about to question anything he said. After all, he *was* the most famous crime fighter in the world. If he believed it, it must be fact.

She turned to Robin. "Pardon me for saying so, but this sort of thing always looked so hard to me. The scaling, I mean. It's rather easy, isn't it?"

Robin shot her a sober look. "Crime fighter's rule number one. Never say that."

"Why?" she asked.

Abruptly, a squad of ice-climbing thugs poured over the ledge above them, suspended on ropes. And as they slid down, their guns barked fiery death.

"That's why," Robin told her.

One of the shooters came flying down his rope right at them, his gun blazing. Robin swung wide on his line, grabbed Batgirl, and pulled her out of the line of fire. Hitting a snowbank, they let go of their ropes and rolled one over the other.

Batgirl was nervous—but she tried not to show it. "Does this mean we're going steady?" she asked Robin, looking into his eyes with a show of merry bravado.

She'd barely gotten the words out before four Icemen landed in the snow beside them. Their guns were drawn, their barrels steaming.

Batgirl caught sight of Batman up on another ledge, a higher one just below the observatory. He was going nose to nose with another squad of Icemen—and holding his own, from the look of it.

More than I can say for us, Batgirl sighed inwardly. Surrounded by the Icemen, she and Robin moved back-to-back. Their enemies leered, savoring the moment of their demise.

"Crime fighter's rule number two," said Robin.

"I'm afraid to ask," she responded.

"Be ready for anything."

Then he did the last thing she would have expected. He put his hands together and yelled, the echo shooting up the hill. A tremendous rumbling came back to them—and a cantilevered overhang of snow collapsed on some of the Icemen, burying them.

Batgirl smiled. The odds still weren't very good—but they were good enough. As Robin did a standing backflip into the thugs directly behind him, she chose the low road—and, pivoting on the heel of her hand, took out a couple more with a leg sweep.

"Pow!" she said, kicking another thug. She socked another. "Wham!" And backhanded a third. "Kazow!"

Robin looked at her. "What are you doing?"

She shrugged. "I don't know. It just feels right."

Slowly but surely, she and Robin began fighting their way through the Icemen in the direction of the observatory.

Batman pulled himself up onto the aperture ledge of the observatory, his breath freezing in a cloud about him. Beneath his mask he was perspiring, having expended too much energy on Freeze's Icemen.

Suddenly, he saw two heads pop up at the opposite side of the ledge. He tensed for a moment—until he recognized them as Robin and Batgirl. Dragging themselves up, they joined him.

The giant chamber was empty—eerily so. The telescope had been abandoned, though it was still aimed at Gotham.

"No sign of the snowman," said Batman.

Robin grunted. "Maybe he melted."

"Don't we wish," Batgirl gibed.

Batman spotted the frozen scientists, helpless in their sheaths of ice. Shooting a Batgrapple into the ceiling, he swung across the room toward the tower and dropped a couple of Batcharges at their feet. Then he continued his swing and landed on the telescope platform below.

Robin and Batgirl were right behind him. They landed on the platform a moment after he did.

Up on the tower, the Batcharges began to glow. Their radiating heat started thawing the scientists.

Batgirl turned to him ominously. "I hope you've got

about ten million more of those little toys." She pointed to the digital clock on the telescope's control console.

The time was 11:52.

"Freeze started his barrage about three minutes ago," said Robin. "Eight more and a city full of Gothamites are ice cubes forever."

Batman thought furiously. Then it hit him. "Sunlight could reverse the freezing process."

"Sunrise isn't for five hours," Batgirl reminded him.

Batman glanced at her. "Here."

"But it's morning in the Congo," Robin added, his eyes lighting up.

Batman pointed to a screen showing a series of satellites—the same one the scientists had used for their demonstration at the press conference. "If we could relay the sunlight—"

"From the other side of the equator—" Robin said, continuing Batman's thought.

Batgirl smiled. "It'll take the satellites about a minute to realign, I expect, but . . . damn!"

Robin looked at her. "Damn? Damn is not good."

"Those targeting mirrors are frozen," she said tautly. "The sun-beam won't work without them."

Batman glanced at the two small mirrors sitting on the telescope barrel. Both were encased in ice.

"I'll set the telescope," he decided. "You two thaw the mirrors."

His sidekicks raced out onto the surface of the telescope. Each one pulled a laser from his or her Utility Belt.

"I love this belt," said Batgirl. "Can I get a matching handbag?"

A moment later, their lasers flared, and they began thawing the mirrors. At the same time, Batman turned his attention to the telescope's main control console. He began working the keyboard.

Typing feverishly, he tried to visualize the results of his

efforts. High above the earth, satellite thrusters would be firing. The giant orbital mirrors designed to work with the telescope would be turning . . .

On the monitor in front of him, graphic representations of the satellites were making adjustments to his specifications. He targeted a blinking graphic of Gotham.

Beside him, the digital clock showed 11:54.

Six minutes. No more.

Batman aimed the telescope. But the shaft shuddered with a sudden impact—and the Gotham skyline visible through the crosshairs was obscured by an unexpected blur.

Even before a hand closed like a vise over his windpipe, the Dark Knight had a fair idea what had happened.

It was Freeze. He had dropped from the rafters onto the mighty cylinder and stuck his helmeted face in front of the targeting scope. And then grabbed Batman while he still had the element of surprise.

"Tonight's forecast," the villain laughed, "a Freeze is coming!"

With that, he used his considerable strength to hurl Batman up over his head. The Dark Knight landed on the telescope barrel—just in time to see Freeze reach out with his free hand and yank on the telescope's joystick. The far end of the barrel swung down all of a sudden.

Unable to stop themselves, Robin and Batgirl went tumbling down its length, rolling toward the end and a dizzying drop to the ground below. Batman tumbled as well—but he stopped himself after a moment and spun around, cape billowing behind him.

Freeze was climbing toward the main control console. Batman had to stop him or Gotham City was as good as dead.

But at the same time, Robin and Batgirl were near the end of the telescope. *They* needed his help, too.

There was no way to get to both Freeze and his crime-fighting partners. No way to be in two places at once. Batman had less than a heartbeat to make his decision.

Clenching his jaw, he went after Mr. Freeze.

A moment later, he felt the subtle tilt that told him Robin and Batgirl had slipped off the end of the telescope—and were dropping toward the icy streets of the city. He tried not to let it slow him down.

Up ahead, Freeze was working at the telescope controls. Before Batman could reach him, he hit a switch.

Instantly, the crime fighter realized what his adversary was up to. Freeze was disabling the telescope's target lock. Up in space, thrusters would be quitting. The satellites Batman had realigned would be halting in mid-turn.

With renewed determination, the Dark Knight struggled up the slope of the telescope toward Freeze. Seeing him, the villain pulled the control lever around, causing the telescope to tilt and spin madly.

By then, Freeze's machine had frozen the moisture right out of the air, creating a snowstorm right there in the observatory. It only made it that much more difficult for Batman to hold on.

Slipping, sliding, with nothing to hang on to, the crime fighter lost his perch and fell. As he dropped, he reached out.

And caught hold of the telescope frame.

CHAPTER

18

As Robin plummeted toward Gotham City, his first thought wasn't for himself. It was for Batgirl, who was falling below him.

The wind was whipping at him mercilessly, numbing him, trying to slow him down. Still, he managed to take a Batgrapple out of his Utility Belt and fire it over his head. Before his eyes, the grapple shot up and secured itself in an icy overhang.

As his line began to play out, Robin reached down for Batgirl. She was reaching up for him at the same time. A fortuitous gust of wind brought her closer. His hand was inches from hers, the city coming up fast.

Just a little farther, he told himself. A little farther . . .

Batman used his grip on the frame to flip himself back up onto the wildly spinning telescope. Flattening himself against it, he slithered toward Freeze and the control console.

He tried to distract the villain, take his mind off the

conflict at hand. "Millions will die so you can save on air-conditioning. Isn't that taking self-help a little too far?"

But Freeze wasn't easily distracted. He drew a cryonic pistol and grinned savagely. "We aim to freeze!" he cried. And he fired.

But Batman deflected the blast with his suit armor.

"That's new," observed Freeze.

It was, too. But the crime fighter had known he would need a defense against Freeze's cryo-weapons.

"Let's swing," the villain sneered.

Then he smashed the joystick forward as far as it would go. The telescope's spin accelerated, forcing Batman to cling for all he was worth.

But it wasn't only *his* life on the line. The two scientists, who had finally thawed, were in danger as well. They were standing on the tower platform in pools of water, the massive telescope careening toward them.

And Batman was in no position to do anything about it.

Freeze hadn't actually *intended* to destroy the scientists.

The truth was he'd forgotten about them. All he'd wanted when he hit the joystick was to send Batman flying off the telescope—so he could smash himself on something hard.

On the other hand, Freeze wasn't going to go out of his way to *avoid* hitting the scientists. He would just as soon have worried about an insect as those bespectacled fools.

"This just isn't my day," groaned one of the scientists, as the telescope swung his way.

As it turned out, it didn't hit him. But it *did* crash into the tower a few rungs below him, causing the structure to topple.

Two things happened then. First, the scientists leaped

and somehow managed to land safely on the swinging telescope, where they hung on to the tensioning bar for dear life.

Second, as the tower platform crumpled under the force of the swinging telescope, it fell into the rail of the floor-level telescope platform—the same telescope platform where Freeze was revolving around the room in accordance with the telescope's gyrations, one hand still on the joystick.

Taken by surprise, he was thrown off his feet by the impact. And perhaps more important, he lost his grip on his gun.

Cursing himself for his clumsiness, Freeze scrambled for the gun. Just as his fingers were about to close on it, he saw a dark apparition loom in front of him.

A dark and unfortunately *familiar* apparition.

Batman didn't get there in time to beat Freeze to his gun. But when the villain aimed it at him, he was quick enough to kick it out of his hands.

Weaponless, Freeze leaped at him and the two of them began to wrestle on the twirling telescope platform, pitting strength against strength and spirit against spirit.

It was a battle of titans, of men possessed—though by very different demons. Batman's demon was his hunger for justice, for balance. Freeze's demon was his need to make the world over in his own frigid image.

"You've turned Gotham to ice," the crime fighter grunted—and socked Freeze in the head with a vicious right hook. "You've endangered millions of lives," he snarled—and smashed Freeze with a devastating left.

"But this," he rasped, "is where the Ice Age ends."

Gathering all his strength, the Dark Knight hauled back and delivered a mighty blow, hurling Freeze onto the back of the telescope. Then, before he could recover, Batman turned to the console and began typing out commands.

On the monitor, he could see graphic representations of the satellites flashing green. The word "targeting" strobed in red above them.

According to the clock, it was 11:58.

Two more minutes. Batman typed even faster.

With agonizing slowness, the targeting mirrors overhead opened and began to glow with ambient sunlight. Freeze screamed hideously at the searing touch of the emerging light—

—and plowed into Batman, stunning him, sending him sprawling into the opposite rail. Dazed, Batman looked up in time to see Freeze's fist. The next thing he knew, he was sprawled on the telescope barrel.

As he tried to climb off it, the villain kicked him hard in the face. As the telescope pitched, Batman fell backward and rolled down its barrel again. He clawed at it, seeking a handhold.

But this time there wasn't any. The frame well out of reach, he continued to slide toward the opening and the cityscape of Gotham many stories below.

Stretching his fingers out as far as they would go, Robin took hold of Batgirl's hand—just as she fired a Bat-grapple from her wrist.

A moment later, Robin's tether pulled tight, wrenching horribly at his shoulder. But somehow he found the strength to hold fast—both to Batgirl and their lifeline.

The two of them dangled over the frigid city, suspended by a tether thinner than his finger. "I've got you," he told her.

Robin had saved her. Just as Dick had saved Barbara

when it looked like she would go over the side of that bridge, back at the motorcycle race.

But then, that's what he did. It was his job. He saved people.

He was still thinking that when his grapple ripped loose from the melting shelf of ice high above them—and suddenly, they were plummeting just as fast as before. For a moment, Robin thought they'd had it.

Then Batgirl's grapple hit the metal roof near their heads and held firm, jerking her upward. At the last possible fraction of a second, she reached out and grabbed him by the wrist.

Now it was Batgirl's tether that pulled tight against her supple strength, her hanging on to it their only chance of survival.

He could see her grimace as she felt his weight drag her down. But she wasn't letting go. He could see it in her eyes.

"No," she groaned as they dangled there. "I've . . . got . . . *you*."

Then, with a mighty effort, she pulled him up to eye level. He grabbed her and held on for dear life, his face inches from hers.

"We've got to stop meeting like this," he told her.

Batman was sliding helplessly toward the slot in the observatory dome—the one through which the telescope projected. He could see the lights of Gotham along the river far below.

He wasn't going to die that way, he told himself. Not tonight. He had too much to do, too many people depending on him.

As Batman slipped out into the night, a frigid wind whipping at him, he pressed his cheek, his gloves, his knees against the barrel of the telescope. Gradually, inch by painful inch, he slowed himself—until it looked like he might have a fighting chance of surviving this.

But the end was looming—literally. Another few feet and he'd go plummeting the way Robin and Batgirl had plummeted. Except with the direction in which the telescope was pointed now, there would be no city beneath him—only the jagged rocks by the river.

Come on, Batman told himself, the wind shrieking all around him. *Come on.*

And then, miracle of miracles, he stopped himself—less than a foot from the bitter end. He took a breath, let it out.

"Wow," said a nearby voice, just audible over the howling of the wind. "Batman."

He turned and saw the two observatory scientists clinging to a targeting groove along the body of the telescope. They looked frazzled but secure enough. And his presence seemed to have had a calming influence.

"I've seen you on TV," one of them said. "Something that *might* have been you, anyway. My friends told me you didn't exist."

Batman glanced down the length of the telescope barrel. At the other end, Freeze was working his way back to the control panel. Knowing how little time he had, the crime fighter glanced at the scientists again.

"Can you give me any more height on this thing?" he asked.

One of the scientists reached down and grabbed a red emergency lever. "Going up," he said.

Then he pulled the lever and the telescope swung straight up, sending Batman soaring through the frigid night toward the stately observatory dome. Flipping in midair, he aimed for the slot made for the telescope . . .

. . . and Freeze, who was visible through the aperture.

But he wasn't going to make it. The Dark Knight could see that with his practiced eye. He was going to fall short of the opening, if only by a few inches. And in this case, a miss was as good as a mile.

Then he remembered something someone had taught him once. A young athlete, with his perfect life stretched out ahead of him, had shared with him his secret strategy in the long jump—a strategy that had won him the decathlon at the Olympic Games.

"I don't land," he had said. "I just *hang* there."

Batman concentrated on that. He focused on it as hard as he'd focused on anything in his life. And just as that young athlete had recommended, he didn't land. He just *hung* there . . .

. . . and hung there . . .

. . . and hung there some more . . .

. . . long enough to make it through the slot and come down on the man who'd given him that advice.

Unable to stand under the weight of Batman's descent, Freeze crashed over the edge of the control platform and into the freezing engine. In the process, his antithermal suit was ripped open.

In that moment, despite the villain's best efforts, the mirrors overhead moved into alignment. The beams of reflected sunlight hit the freezing engine. And Freeze was struck by the rays as well, forced to watch as they penetrated his damaged suit.

The telescope was alive with power all of a sudden, an intense thawing beam shooting from its giant lens. Batman turned to Freeze, who was beginning to turn gray and wither.

"You're losing your cool," he said.

Freeze's lip curled in disdain. "I think not. There'll be no hot time in this old town tonight." He produced a remote control device. "You'll get a charge out of this, my friend."

Pressing a button on the device, he rolled out of the sunlight and fell to the floor. Suddenly, a series of explosions in quick succession wracked the area around the base of the telescope. And with each rapid-fire impact, the giant instrument tore loose of its moorings a little more.

Finally, with a scream of twisting metal and cracking concrete, it slid through its slot altogether, taking Batman, the telescope platform, and a chunk of observatory floor along with it—not to mention the two scientists clinging to the targeting groove.

Together, they began to fall, headed for the frozen river-bank and certain death on the rocks below.

As the wind ripped past him, stinging his eyes merci-lessly, Batman's first thought was to get to the scientists. If he could reach them, he might be able to save their lives.

Sliding down the telescope from the control platform—yet again—he simultaneously sought out the one structure he knew he could count on.

And found it.

Aiming the launcher mounted on his wrist, he fired a double-ended Bat-tether and watched twin grapples shoot horizontally into the air . . . then sink into the arms of the giant sculpture holding up the observatory as the telescope plummeted past.

Batgirl was just helping Robin onto an icy ledge be-neath the slot in the observatory dome when they heard—no, felt—a series of explosions. A moment later, the giant telescope, carrying Batman and two other men, plunged past them.

"Now, that," said her companion, his voice taut with concern, "is what I call an exit."

The sight of their friend and two innocents falling to their deaths was a compelling, even horrific spectacle. But Batgirl had barely noticed it before something else cap-tured her attention.

Looking past Robin, she cursed softly. "Please tell me he's on our side," she said, gazing at the mammoth, muscle-bound monstrosity.

But with his leather mask and the tubes leading from the back of his head, he didn't look like anyone she wanted to meet in a dark alley, much less in the skies over Gotham.

"His name is Bane," said Robin.

He coiled and leaped into a spinning roundhouse kick. But the man called Bane knocked him away with a backhanded blow, sending him flying into a snowdrift.

Then the giant began advancing on Batgirl.

She went into a flurry of action, letting Bane have it with a series of punches and kicks. Her whole arsenal, in fact. Unfortunately, it didn't do any good. He might as well have been made of steel.

Out of the corner of her eye, she saw Robin stand up. "Don't worry," she grunted. "I've got him."

Just then, Bane grabbed her by the throat and slammed her into an ice wall. Her senses left her for a moment. When they came back again, she could taste blood in her mouth—and see Bane bringing his fist back in preparation for a killing blow.

"No," she heard Robin say. "*I've* got him."

Turning, she saw her companion leap into the air—and rip away the tubes connecting Bane's injector pack to the back of his skull. As the tubes flapped about, a milky substance sprayed wildly into the air, hissing where it made contact with the snow.

Bane released Batgirl and hit the ledge, writhing. He seemed to be getting smaller, less muscular, as she looked on—shrinking, amazing as it sounded. After just a few seconds, the man was a scrawny shadow of his former self, struggling in the folds of his costume.

"You should get that suit taken in," Robin gibed as he

grabbed a fistful of Bane's vest. "No one's buying baggy anymore."

As Batman clung to the telescope, he saw the jagged rocks alongside the river rush up at him with dizzying speed. But if he was discomfited by the sight, the scientists were absolutely terrified.

"Grab my belt," he roared over the rush of the wind, "and hang on."

Frantic with fear, the scientists did as they were told. In fact, they were only too glad to latch on to something, anything, no matter how fragile a chance it might be.

A moment later, Batman's grappling cable pulled taut.

The crime fighter felt a tremendous jolt of pain in his right shoulder as he assumed the weight of three grown men, the telescope dropping out beneath them like the trapdoor in a giant gallows.

As Batman and the scientists continued to sink, bending the cable like a bowstring in the hands of a titanic archer, the pain in his shoulder became an electric agony.

But still he held on, jaw clenched, fighting his way past his misery until the three of them reached their lowest point—over an outcropping of rock on the cliff face below the observatory.

Below, the telescope hit the rocks and exploded in a conflagration that threw the cliffs into stark relief. For a split second, Batman experienced a pang of grief for the thing. He—or rather, Bruce Wayne—had meant it to be a symbol of hope. And now it was dashed.

But it was just a symbol. Batman wouldn't believe *real* hope had died along with it.

"This is your stop," he told the scientists.

Freeing himself from their grasps, first one and then the other, he saw them drop safely onto a ledge just a few feet below them. Then, the weight on it reduced dramatically, Batman felt the cable go taut again—propelling him back up toward the observatory like a straight, dark arrow.

Once again, his shoulder was punished—this time by the force of acceleration. Once again, it stood the test.

The Batman soared toward the thickening, gray clouds, past the mammoth statue holding up the observatory. At precisely the right moment, he pressed a stud on his wrist-launcher and allowed the cable ends to spring free.

Then he continued his flight unrestricted. Almost immediately, he could feel gravity resume its claim on him. But by then, he was already shooting past the observatory.

Knowing he would have only one chance to perform this maneuver, Batman concentrated on getting it right. As he ascended past the observatory, he twisted in midair and spread his cape, using every tool at his disposal to change the direction of his flight.

Then, with an ease that belied the magnitude of his effort, he flipped neatly through the slot formerly occupied by the telescope and landed on the observatory floor.

And he wasn't alone. No sooner had he completed his vault than he saw Robin and Batgirl flip through the slot as well. They had made it—*all* of them.

Robin grinned. "Winded, old-timer?"

Batman didn't give him the satisfaction of frowning at him. "Don't make me kill you in front of the girl," he said.

As one, they approached the rubble-strewn control console. Its chronometer was still intact. But the news it gave them wasn't good.

"It's almost midnight," Batgirl pointed out. "And the telescope's gone. There's no way to thaw the city."

Batman stroked his chin. There *was* a way, he insisted, wracking his brain for one. There was *always* a way.

Then he hit on it.

"Theoretically," he said, "the satellites could be positioned to thaw the city directly. But it would take a computer genius." He eyed his companions. "Know anyone who fits that description?"

"I'm on it," said Robin.

Clearing the debris away from the console, he began to type. But to no avail. The equipment was dead inside.

"No," said Batgirl, shouldering Robin aside. "*I'm* on it."

She located a couple of broken wires and quick-patched them. Suddenly, the console sprang to life. Without missing a beat, she began hacking.

"Ms. Genius," she muttered, without looking up. "Madame Genius. Her Geniusness. Which sounds better?"

Batman took a closer look at the monitor. According to the graphics, the giant orbital satellites were beginning to align.

He imagined a full disk of the sun appearing in the mirror of one satellite. He imagined that solar energy reflected from the first satellite to the second one, and then to the one after that and the one after that, until the last unit in the string beamed a ray of hot, pure sunlight at Gotham.

Suddenly, Batman saw a glint in the dense, gray sky, an ember of faith among the ashes of his city's despair. As he watched, the ember became a glow, then a narrow, red-gold shaft of light. Then several shafts of light, cutting through the cloud cover like a celestial cavalry.

The giant rays of focused sunlight played over the city. And whatever they touched, they warmed. Slowly, inexorably, life was restored to the frozen canyons of Gotham.

As the beams of sunlight hit the base of the observatory, the ice began to melt off it. The entire cliff was thawing, its frigid sheath running in rivulets down to the river.

Only then did Batman give a thought to Freeze. Turning, he saw his adversary lying amid the rubble, weak and gray with the growing heat. The villain was straining just to breathe.

Batman walked over and knelt beside him.

Freeze looked up at him with hate in his eyes. "Go on," he rasped. "Kill me too . . . just as you killed my wife."

Batman shook his head. "I didn't kill your wife." He pressed a button on his Utility Belt to provide proof of his claim. "Run Ivy evidence tape 001.40."

Then he showed Freeze a tiny monitor in his gauntlet, which displayed an image of Poison Ivy. "As I told Lady Freeze when I pulled her plug," Ivy was saying, "this is a one-woman show."

Freeze's eyes opened wide. He screamed his rage, his face streaming with frozen tears like tiny diamonds.

"But Ivy never killed her," Batman assured him. "Your wife isn't dead, Victor. She's alive."

Freeze's eyes narrowed. "How . . . ?"

"We found her," Batman said. "Just in time, apparently. And we restored her icy slumber."

He spoke a new command and his gauntlet monitor switched images. Now it showed Freeze's mate, sleeping once again in cryogenic peace.

"You see? She's still frozen," he told the former scientist. "Still waiting for you to find a cure for her disease."

Freeze breathed a sigh of relief. "Still frozen," he echoed, turning his face away. "Still alive."

Batman saw his chance then. It was still a long shot. But it was also his *only* shot.

"I know what it's like to lose everything you've ever loved," he said.

Freeze regarded him, looking for a lie in his face. But he wouldn't find one, Batman knew. After all, he *did* know what it was like.

"But vengeance isn't power," he went on. "Any two-bit thug with a gun can take a life. To give life . . . that's true power. A power you once had."

Freeze was listening to him. For now, that was all he could hope for.

"I don't know if you'll ever find a cure for your wife," Batman told him. "But I'm asking you now, Dr. Victor Fries, to save another life. Show me how to cure McGregor's Syndrome, stage one. And maybe you can also save the man your wife once loved—a man who's buried deep inside you."

Batman paused, hoping he'd been persuasive enough. He looked into his adversary's eyes, into his soul, hoping he was right about what was buried there.

"Will you help me, Doctor?"

Freeze stared at Batman. Emotions moved across his face like summer storms. Finally, he unsealed his chestplate, removed two glowing power orbs, and held them out in his hand. His smile was bittersweet.

"Take two of these," he said, "and call me in the morning."

Accepting the orbs, Batman made a call to the cops over his cowl radio. But Freeze stopped him and asked for a favor.

Knowing Freeze's villainy had been broken, Batman was tempted to grant it. But he couldn't.

Still, he had a feeling Freeze would find a way to get what he wanted all on his own.

CHAPTER

19

Poison Ivy sat in a barred square of moonlight in her cell at Arkham Asylum, considering the tiny flower she held in her hand.

She could hear the shrieking and cursing that came from the cells of her fellow inmates farther down the corridor. The Riddler, the Mad Hatter, Maxie Zeus . . . all of them thoroughly mad. All of them hollowed out by this place until they were devoid of hope.

Only the Scarecrow refrained from shrieking and cursing with the rest of them. But he was the maddest of all.

In the whole cellblock, perhaps in the whole asylum, only Ivy was able to cling to her sanity. And what made her different? she asked herself. What made her unique here?

The promise that still lay like a seedling in her breast. The anticipation of spring, lush and green and sweet-smelling, rolling over humankind like a mighty, flower-covered steamroller.

That, and a more personal hope.

She turned to the window, wondering how long it would be until winter arrived. Then she began pulling the petals out of the flower, one by one.

"He loves me," she said, her words little more than a sigh. "He loves me not. He loves me. He loves me—"

"Not," a voice interrupted, followed by a click as of a lock opening.

Ivy turned and saw a figure cloaked in shadows. It stepped forward, revealing itself as Mr. Freeze.

"It's amazing what you can buy around here for a few dozen diamonds," he told her.

He approached her. Coldly, she thought. But that was hardly a surprise. His aloofness, his hard-to-get quality was one of the things she found attractive about him.

"Freeze," she said. "I knew you'd come to get me. The same way I came to get you." Caught up in the nearness of him, she reached up as if to stroke his cheek right through his helmet.

Before she could touch him, however, he grabbed her wrist. His mouth twisted with rage.

"I didn't have enough to buy my way out of here," he grated. His eyes narrowed savagely. "Just *in.*"

"In?" she echoed. "But why . . . ?"

And suddenly, she knew. Somehow, Freeze had found out about his wife—the way she'd *really* died, at Ivy's hands.

She became afraid. *Very* afraid.

"Prepare for a bitter harvest," Freeze told her, his eyes glinting like daggers. "Winter has come at last."

Ivy swallowed. This wasn't the kind of cold embrace she'd had in mind.

Bruce watched morning break in the hills to the east, a glow of ruddy gold sandwiched between the horizon and an unbroken blanket of clouds. Then he turned away from the window to look back over his shoulder.

The living room of stately Wayne Manor was filled with

pizza boxes, Chinese food containers, and articles of cloth-
ing strewn over the furniture. Barbara, who had been up
half the night watching over her uncle, was dozing on the
couch. Dick was pacing, red-eyed with lack of sleep himself.

They were afraid, all of them. Afraid that Alfred would
be lost to them forever. But Bruce was afraid the *most*.

After all, Alfred had been his world for a very long and
very vulnerable time. In a way, losing the old man would
be like losing his parents all over again. And he didn't
know how he would be able to endure that.

Bruce squinted as the sun blazed forth, revealed in all
its glory. Then that glory faded as it rose out of view behind the clouds.

In the distance, he saw a V-shaped flock of geese. They
were headed for warmer climes—unlike the bats in the
caverns below the house, who remained all year long in
their chittering darkness.

As he followed the geese's flight, Bruce was reminded
of a day long ago. He saw himself as a boy again, standing
outside on the estate's snow-dusted fields, trying to imagine what Alfred could be saying to the stout man in the
living room.

It wasn't until the following week that he realized the
man was a psychiatrist. A psychiatrist, in fact, who meant
to relieve him of the pain he was feeling as a result of his
parents' deaths.

There had been just one problem. Bruce hadn't *wanted*
to be relieved of the pain. It was all he still had of Martha
and Thomas Wayne and he wasn't about to give it up.

Of course, the stout man wouldn't have accepted that.
Even at his tender age, young Bruce knew that with grim
certainty. There was only one way the stout man would
leave him alone.

So Bruce opened up to him—or pretended to. He poured
out his feelings of loneliness, of rage, of fear and resent-

ment. Or rather, not his real feelings, but what he thought the stout man wanted to hear.

It pleased the stout man no end that he had cured the boy. He had gone into the arrangement believing Bruce was a hopeless case, but somehow he had drawn him out. In fact, he'd told Alfred that it was one of the highlights of his career as a therapist.

Of course, Alfred had known what was going on. But he hadn't intervened to protest the boy's behavior. It was as if he'd sensed that Bruce would need a clean bill of health one day. As if he'd known the boy would need to fade into the background, bland and uninteresting, so someone else could emerge and never be linked to him.

Before the eyes of the adult Bruce, the flock of geese vanished past the treetops. He sighed. *Alfred . . .*

Suddenly, he heard a harrumph. It had come from the vicinity of the stairs. By the look on his face, Dick had heard it, too.

Rousing Barbara, practically lifting her off the couch, Bruce and Dick made for the hallway. But before they could get there, they saw someone walking toward them from the other direction.

Two someones, actually. As Bruce watched, a lump taking hold in his throat, he saw that one of them was Alfred. The other was Doc Simpson, holding Alfred's arm for support. But mostly it was the old butler, scowling as he went, who was doing the work of transporting himself.

Simpson let go of the man, and Alfred took the last few steps into the room by himself. And there was some color in his face, by God. He looked as if he'd gotten some of his old strength back.

Barbara blinked at the sight of her uncle. She peered at him with disbelieving eyes. Dick was staring, too, not daring to ask the question to which they all wanted to know the answer.

In the end, it was Bruce who asked it. Sort of.

"Alfred," he said, despite the tightness in his throat. "Are you . . . ?"

The butler's scowl deepened. "Rather disappointed at how poorly I seem to have taught you proper housekeeping?" He glanced disapprovingly around the room. "Why, yes, I am."

Alfred allowed himself a bit of a smile. "And quite well, it seems. Thanks to you, Master Bruce. Thanks to you all."

Bruce went over to him. So did Dick and Barbara. One by one, they hugged the man who was at the center of their family. The man who held it all together for them.

"Well," said Simpson, "I ought to be going now. But I'll stop by later to check in." He paused for a moment to shake his head. "I don't know where Wayne Industries had to go to get that antigen, Bruce—or who you got it from. But it's going to save a lot of people a lot of misery."

The billionaire smiled. "When administered by dedicated and caring physicians. Thanks for all your help, Doctor."

Nodding, Simpson left. Alfred moved a pizza carton with thinly veiled repugnance and sat on the couch where Barbara had been sleeping. He eyed his niece with curiosity.

"You know," he told her, "I had the most remarkable dream while I was convalescing. I dreamed that while I was asleep, you had hacked your way into the disc I specifically forbade you to look at."

Barbara flushed. "Er . . . right. Well, you see, I—"

"And that's not all," Alfred said. "I dreamed that you took that proprietary knowledge and used it to create a suit. A *Bat*suit, of all things. And then you used your new autumn apparel to go after Poison Ivy." He chuckled. "It's amazing how foolish you can be when you're dreaming."

Barbara swallowed. "You overheard us talking, didn't you? When we thought you were still asleep?"

Dick grunted. "Nothing gets past good ol' Al. *Nothing.*"

Bruce moved the pizza box a little farther along the length of the couch and sat beside Alfred. "Welcome back," he told his friend.

"It's good to be back," said Alfred.

Dick pointed at Bruce. "I've been meaning to ask you something. When Barbara . . . er, Batgirl and I rolled off the telescope, you didn't try to save us." He tilted his head. "How come? It was the first time I ever fell and you weren't there to catch me."

Bruce shrugged. "I knew you could handle it," he said easily.

"You did?" Barbara asked.

Dick shot her a look. She noticed it.

"I mean," she added quickly, "of course you did."

"Sometimes," said Bruce, "counting on someone else is the only way to win." He winked at Dick. "At least, that's what I've heard."

Barbara appeared indignant suddenly. "Hey, I'm the one who kicked Ivy's botanical butt. Personally. Me. I did."

Bruce looked at her askance. "Yes, you did," he agreed. "And you'll have plenty of time to savor the experience back at school."

She stared at him. "School? After all we've been through together, you'd send me back to that place?"

Dick rolled his eyes. "Give up, Bruce. This is one argument you're never going to win." He glanced at Alfred. "You either, Al."

Barbara clapped Dick on the shoulder. "I knew there was a reason I saved you from certain death."

Dick turned to her. "*You* saved *me*?"

She nodded. "As I recall, yes."

He thought about it for a moment. "Maybe you did at that."

Barbara extended her hand. "Partners?"

Robin clasped her offering. "Partners," he confirmed. Then the two of them turned to Bruce.

He stood, sighed, and enveloped both their hands in his own. *Why fight the inevitable?* he thought. "Partners."

Alfred smiled from his place on the couch. "I do believe we're going to need a bigger cave."

"You can worry about that later," said Bruce. "Right now, you need to get some rest."

Alfred held up his hand. "If it's all right with you, sir, I'd like to stay right here. I've had enough bed rest to last me a lifetime."

"Hey, look," said Barbara, facing the windows that looked toward Gotham. She pointed to the sky. "The Bat-Signal."

Bruce turned and saw it emblazoned on the blanket of clouds. They appeared to have thickened and darkened over the last few minutes, as if gathering for some mighty outburst.

A storm coming, he thought. In Gotham, it seemed, there was *always* a storm coming. But this time, he wouldn't have to weather it alone.

He took some comfort in that as he headed for the grandfather clock that led down to the Batcave . . . with Dick and Barbara close on his heels.

Warner Books now offers an exciting range of quality titles by both established and new authors. All of the books in this series are available from:

Little, Brown and Company (UK),
P.O. Box 11,
Falmouth,
Cornwall TR10 9EN.

Fax No: 01326 317444.
Telephone No: 01326 372400
E-mail: books@barni.avel.co.uk

Payments can be made as follows: cheque, postal order (payable to Little, Brown and Company) or by credit cards, Visa/Access. Do not send cash or currency. UK customers and B.F.P.O. please allow £1.00 for postage and packing for the first book, plus 50p for the second book, plus 30p for each additional book up to a maximum charge of £3.00 (7 books plus).

Overseas customers including Ireland, please allow £2.00 for the first book plus £1.00 for the second book, plus 50p for each additional book.

NAME (Block Letters) ....

....

ADDRESS ....

....

....

☐ I enclose my remittance for ....

☐ I wish to pay by Access/Visa Card

Number

Card Expiry Date